Where the Lilies Cry

By

C. Stephen Badgley

Cover Art by

Mary Louise Holt

Badgley Publishing Company

ISBN NUMBER 978-0-9854403-6-7

This book is dedicated to my Sister-In Law

Joyce Arlene Gloeckner Badgley

Whose words of encouragement prompted and inspired me to continue to write.

Prologue

Crouched behind the upturned roots of a fallen tree, the frontiersman pursed his lips and made the sounds of a turkey gobbling. He mimicked the bird perfectly. He was attempting to lure a Shawnee hunter close to his position. He saw the lone figure approach through the shaded woods, bent over and moving slowly.

Studying the ground for signs of his quarry the hunter did not notice the frontiersman laying in ambush. The frontiersman waited quietly as the Indian moved passed him. When the Indian was about ten feet away, he leapt from his hiding place and threw his tomahawk with all his might at the back of the unsuspecting warrior.

The hawk sailed through the air and the blade struck deep into the hunter just below his shoulder blades. As the Indian sank to his knees, the frontiersman pulled his knife from the sheath on his belt and raced towards the falling warrior. He grabbed the hair of his victim just as he was falling forward and pulling his head back, he sliced through the warrior's throat.

With blood spurting from his dying prey, he cut a deep circle on top of the Indian's head. Tossing his knife to the ground, he grabbed the Indian's hair with both hands and put his foot on the warrior's back. He yanked backwards as he kicked the Indian forward and the scalp separated from the skull with a loud sucking sound.

Dying, the warrior rolled over to look at his attacker. He knew who he was before he looked. The frontiersman put his foot on the Indian's chest and standing there holding the bloody scalp skyward, let out a long, loud piercing scream that echoed through the surrounding hills. He knelt down beside the Indian and watched him die.

A quarter mile away, three Shawnee warriors had just gotten a fire started and were awaiting their brother's return when the strange scream reverberated through the woods, one of them immediately threw his blanket over the fire to extinguish it. They looked at one another apprehensively and began to gather their belongings. They knew their brother was dead. They knew that unearthly sound was created by the supernatural being they had been sent to kill. They called him The Death Wind for after he killed he would announce his victory to the world with his blood curdling scream.

His real name was Lewis Wetzel and he was responsible for the death of so many Indians that their Chief had ordered them to find him and kill him. Others had come before them, but none were successful for Lewis Wetzel was a better woodsman and warrior than any Indian or white man that ever lived. He also seemed to have a sixth sense that warned him of the presence of enemies out to get him.

Unbeknownst to the warriors, Wetzel had been tracking them for days, waiting for his chance to strike. The warriors were doomed from the moment he laid eyes on them and now, with their presence discovered, they knew they would probably never see their village again. All they could do was separate and try to make it back to their village alive. It would be just a matter time before Wetzel caught and killed each one for he would never give up in his quest to kill as many Indians as he could.

Long before the State of Ohio existed, the lands there were considered "wilderness" by the colonists in the east, inhabited by "ignorant savages" and wild animals.

The people of the Ohio Country were far from being ignorant and the term savage could be applied to both Indians and whites as they both committed horrible acts against one another.

Along the beautiful Ohio River just below the falls in the Great Bend was a small village named Quenolapay Ohtenatit or Little Buck Town. It was inhabited by people of the Shawnee Nation and the Lenape or Delaware Nation. The Shawnee considered the Lenape their grandfathers.

Across the river on the Virginia side was a trading post set up and run by James Letort with the backing of the West Jersey Trading Company in Philadelphia.

James Letort Sr. was the son of James I and Ann Letort, pioneers of the trading business in Pennsylvania. The older James had come to America with his father to escape persecution in France. They were protestant Huguenots and declared their loyalty to the British Crown. The older James died and his sons carried on the trading business under the auspices of their mother Ann.

James Letort Sr. was an exceptional trader who had a reputation of dealing fair with all Indians. As a young man he was adopted into the Shawnee nation. He married a Shawnee woman and had a son whom they named James Letart Jr. The name Letort was changed to Letart, probably because of the constant mispronunciation of the name by the English.

This work is a combination of historical fact and fiction created to give the reader an idea of what life was possibly like in the sometimes turbulent era of the Ohio Frontier.

Chapter 1

1704

James Letort stood before the Council at Philadelphia and stated, "I do not understand why you have called me here, why you doubt my loyalty. I have done nothing to warrant this inquisition. I am a protestant just as you are! The French Catholic king murdered my family years ago! My father escaped and came to the new world where we could live our lives without persecution for our beliefs. I was born here, a British subject just as you!"

Although my heritage is French I have nothing but hatred for them and what they stand for. Five years ago, I was taken captive by them. They sent me to Tholoun where they were going to hang me for my refusal to declare allegiance to their government. I managed to escape and made my way to England where I contracted with the West Jersey Company to trade with the Indians. I have been their agent since and all of my dealings have been with the English."

"Mr. Letort," said one of the magistrates, "We are not here to persecute or prosecute you. We know that what you have stated is true. This Council was called because we feel there are some questions that need to be asked. What was your reasoning to journey to Canada last year?"

"I went there to settle some accounts, pay some debts I owed and collect some debts owed me."

"If you deal only with English concerns as you just stated, why did you have debts and collections with the French in Canada?"

"The debts I owed were incurred by my father years ago. I went to Canada on his behalf to settle the accounts of the kind people who helped our family to escape from France. The debts I went to collect were owed me and my associates by French traders and Indians that occurred when I first started trading long ago. I would have forgone the latter, but was induced by my associates to at least attempt to collect these debts. I was successful in both endeavors and will have no further dealings with any of them. I have always been faithful and bore true allegiance to the Crown of England and I am ready to give such further security as should be thought reasonable."

"Mr. Letort, While you were in Canada did you hear of any French intentions to influence the Indians in Pennsylvania? There have been reports that they have stepped up their efforts to induce the Indians here about to raise the tomahawk against us. Did you hear anything that could confirm these reports?"

"I heard nothing. The people I dealt with were farmers and traders. I had no dealings with anyone in the French government or military. The traders were very aloof and were not happy to see me and they shared no intelligence with me. The Indians I met with reacted in the same way. I did not ask any questions in regards to French intentions. I was mainly concerned with procuring debts owed me and my associates. Had I heard any news of this nature, I would surely have reported it to the authorities upon my return."

"The Council will now retire to consider your testament and the testament of others. We will also consider reports we have received against you. We will convene on the morrow. You will be brought forth and be advised of our findings. You will be held in the jail until that time. Guards! Remove Mr. Letort to the jail. See that he is well treated! Bring forth Peter Bassillion!"

James was escorted to the jail and as he was placed in his cell he asked the guard for quill and parchment to write a letter. His wife Ann was standing outside the jail and he requested she be allowed to enter. The guard brought quill, ink and paper to James and went to fetch his wife. James sat down and began to write:

To Mr. Adam Miller, West Jersey Trading Company

My Dear Mr. Miller,

As I write this letter, I am sitting in the jail under order of the Council. Apparently, because I am of French descent and journeyed to Canada last year, they are in doubt concerning the loyalty of myself and my associates to the British Crown. I assure you sir, that myself, Bassillion and Chartier are loyal British subjects and in no way would we ever align ourselves with the French Government.

I am writing this letter to beg for your assistance in this matter. I know not what the Council will proclaim on the morrow, but undoubtedly they will ask for security. I have some funds but they are limited. Perhaps if you would attend tomorrow's Council and help us defend our good names the Council will be lenient in their judgment. I am sending this letter by my wife Ann. Please give her your reply.

Your most humble servant,
James Letort

James folded the letter and handed it to his wife. "Ann, take this to Mr. Miller at the Company. I have asked him to give you a letter of reply. Make haste."

"I will take it James, and I tell you if no good comes from this and the Council decides to punish you further, I will myself journey to Canada to my brothers in Quebec. We will raise a force such as never seen before in this land to free you. We will kill every one of those English bastards on the Council."

"Ann, watch your tongue! You will do no such thing. Don't ever say anything like that again. If you are heard speaking such things, our lives will be worth nothing! I swear woman, you are going to be the death of me. You must learn to control your anger! Now take this letter and wait for a reply."

In a huff, Ann took the letter and left the jail. She mounted her horse and rode through the streets of Philadelphia to the West Jersey Trading Company office. Dismounting, she hurried to the door and knocked loudly. An elderly gentleman opened the door and bade her to enter.

"Mrs. Letort...so happy to see you! What word on your husband's dealings with the Council? All is well I pray."

"All is not well! The Council is to meet again tomorrow. Here is a letter from my husband to you Mr. Miller and he asks that I wait for a reply."

Mr. Miller took the letter from Ann and sat down at a table and began to read. When he was finished reading, he turned the letter over and began to write on the back:

My Dear Mr. Letort,

Of course I will be present tomorrow at the Council and you are to have no worries concerning the outcome. I will beg for your immediate release from incarceration and whatever amount of security the Council demands will be met. You will pay whatever you can and the Company will make up the difference.

You and your associates are the best agents this Company has and we will do everything possible to return you and your friends to your labors.

Your Humble Servant,
Adam Miller

He folded the paper and handed it to Ann. "Not to worry Ann, we will see that your husband and the others are set free. You take this letter to your husband and assure him that I will be there tomorrow."

Chapter Two

The old warrior Chingwe, The Bobcat, dipped his paddle into the water of the gently flowing river and guided his canoe towards the northern shore. In the canoe with him were his grandchildren, Blue Feather, his beautiful eleven year old granddaughter and his two grandsons Dark Sky and Gray Squirrel, ages ten and eight.

It was early summer, the morning sun was just beginning to rise over the top of the hills and a light fog was swirling over the dark green water as they glided across the surface of the river.

Shiner minnows attempting to escape from feeding bass and crappie, sprayed out of the water along the shores as these predators rushed into the schools to grab a minnow. Sand Hill cranes and other feeding birds stalked the edge of the water along the shore trying to grab an unsuspecting frog or minnow.

"Look Grandfather! Isn't the sun beautiful this morning, its turning the sky so red!" exclaimed Blue Feather. "It's going to be a wonderful day isn't it Grandfather?"

"Looks like rain." answered the old man.

Dark Sky who was sitting in the bow of the canoe turned to his Grandfather and exclaimed, "Look Grandfather, see that big rock on the shoreline over there! I just saw a big white bird take off from the top of it."

"That is where we are going Dark Sky, this place we called Sikona Yapewi. When I was just a young boy, my friends and I used to come here to fish and swim. I want to show you something."

The huge rock towered above them as the old warrior guided the canoe to the base of a huge boulder that had come loose from the hills many, many years ago. It had rolled down the hill and settled right on the bank of the river. It had split during its descent and a large flat piece of it settled in the water next to it.

The old man was scanning the rock with his eyes, looking for something.

"Look! It is still here, time has not erased it. Here, children, is my sign. I put this here when I was not much older than you are now."

The children gazed up at the carved image of a bobcat that had been meticulously engraved into the stone by their Grandfather.

"And here are the signs of my friends, Waupee the White Hawk and Toti, the Frog." He chuckled as he reminisced about his friends.

"Why are you laughing Grandfather?" asked Gray Squirrel.

"I was just remembering my friend Toti and thinking of the first time we came to this place. Toti was a Lenape, a Delaware. The Lenape are the grandfathers of the Shawnee and we both shared the same village below the falls. My mother was a Delaware."

"Toti's father named him Frog and it was a good name, for he actually looked like a frog! He had long legs and could swim underwater faster than anyone I ever knew. When we first found this place, Toti and my friend White Hawk both ran to the edge of this boulder and dived into the water. They were both treading water and taunting me to jump in when Toti got the strangest look on his face. He began screaming and thrashing around in the water."

"Something is trying to eat me!" he screamed. "He went under the water and came back up holding a catfish about this long." The old man held his hands apart about shoulder width.

"He and White Hawk struggled to get the catfish up on the shore."

"White Hawk said, "Toti, you should not go into the water any more. Catfish like to eat frogs."

"We all had a good laugh. We had that Catfish for a meal and it sure tasted good."

Blue Feather said, "Tell us about your friends and your life here Grandfather. Can we see where your wigwam was?"

"We will first go to where my Grandfather had his trading post. We will make camp near there and I will tell you of this place and your ancestors. We need to get some shelter up before the rain comes."

He began paddling the canoe towards the southern side of the river and upstream. As they rounded a bend the current in the river picked up and they could hear the distant sound of rushing water.

The forest came right down to the river's edge and Chingwe maneuvered the canoe next to the southern shoreline where the current was not as strong and paddling was easier. The sound of the falls became louder the farther upstream they went. Soon they could see the distant falls and the islands. There were several cabins standing on the shore just below the falls. Smoke was drifting from their chimneys wafting slowly upwards into the blue sky.

The water coming over the falls created a fine mist that rose into the air. Chingwe beached the canoe about a quarter mile from the falls on the Virginia shore. He and the children climbed out of the canoe and gathered their supplies. After pulling the canoe up into the woods and covering it with brush, they made their way to find a suitable place to set up camp.

The old warrior noticed a turkey skittering through the woods in front of them and he motioned for the children to get down and be quiet. Taking his rifle he slowly made his way forward. He quietly placed himself behind a fallen tree and pursed his lips making the gobbling sound of a turkey. The turkey, a big male, heard the noise and came to investigate. Chingwe waited until he was within twenty yards and took his head off with a ball from his rifle. They would eat well today.

They found a small clearing in the woods and set up camp. They found an area with four small sapling trees growing close together. Stripping the branches from the saplings, they bent them over and tied the tops together forming a frame upon which they interlaced long limber sticks horizontally and tied spruce branches and some animal hides they had brought with them. They soon had a suitable shelter to seek refuge from the rain and for sleeping.

Chingwe got a fire going and after cleaning the turkey he spitted him on the ramrod from his rifle and began roasting him over the fire. The sun was approaching its midway climb into the heavens and the air was filled with the sweet smell of honeysuckle. The children hadn't eaten much since they left their village on the Scioto. A little dried pemmican and some parched corn was all they had taken with them. The turkey would be a welcome change from that.

After they had eaten, the old Warrior motioned for his grandchildren to follow him. He led back down to the river and began walking upstream towards the rapids. After a short while, he re-entered the woods and they came upon what was left of a fairly large log cabin.

The cabin had been burned some years ago. The only thing standing was the old stone chimney. Digging around the burnt ruins the children found a rusty old beaver trap and an axe head. The old man sat beneath a towering oak tree and reminisced about his youth as the children explored the area.

Blue Feather found some mushrooms growing nearby and soon her basket she always carried was filled with these delicious morsels. Dark Sky had managed to knock a squirrel out of a Hickory Tree with a well thrown rock. They would have a little more fresh meat for their evening repast.

"This was my Grandfather's trading post," The old warrior said as the children returned and sat next to him. "He was a Frenchman and his name was James Letort. The English and the Indians pronounced his name Letart."

"My Grandmother was Pahcotai Koona...Autumn Snow. She was Shawnee and my Grandfather took her as his wife in the Wedding Dance years ago. They had a son whom they named James Letort Jr. His Shawnee name was Cahiktodo. He was my Father."

Many years ago, my Grandfather and his brother Jacques were sent by their Mother, Ann Letort, from Pennsylvania to establish trading posts in these parts. Jacques settled upriver from here, near what the white men today call Ravenswood. My Grandfather came on down river and built his cabin here.

They traveled down the river by flatboat and carried huge quantities of goods which they traded with the Indians for furs of the beaver, otter, mink, deer, bear, buffalo and other animals.

My Grandfather gave up trying to have his name pronounced correctly and settled on the name Letart. After the Indians were forced out of the area and the English settled in on the other side of the river, they called the little town they built Letartsville after my Father. Now it is called Letart Falls, but when I was a child there, we called the village Quenolapay Ohtenatit or Little Buck Town.

I have returned to these places several times since we left and have made friends with some of the white families living near our old village. They have proven to be kind and soon I will visit them again and ask their permission to show you children where your roots are. Let us now return to our camp and I will tell you more of your ancestors before we turn in for the night.

Upon their return to the camp, Blue Feather entered the shelter and came out with a small iron skillet that had been given to her by her Mother. She placed some bear fat into the skillet and sat it on some rocks by the fire her Grandfather made. As the fat began to melt, she cleaned the mushrooms and dropped them into the sizzling fat. The boys had gutted and cleaned the squirrel. They were roasting it over the fire.

The old man was busy rigging up some drop lines to catch some catfish. He had a few metal hooks he had obtained from traders near his village up the Scioto. He attached the hooks to three ten-foot lengths of twine he had also traded for. He baited the hooks with some of the innards from the turkey they had eaten earlier and made his way down towards the river.

When he reached the river's edge he looked for some small saplings growing near the shore. He bent them over and tied the lines to them. Wrapping the other end of the line around a small rock he cast his line into the water. The weight of the rock would keep the bait on the bottom. When a fish took the bait, the line would come away from the rock and the fish would have to battle the whipping motion of the sapling to gain its freedom. The tugging against the sapling's giving and taking motion would soon wear down the fish and reduce the chance of the fish breaking the line. "With any luck" he thought, "We will have some good eating tomorrow."

When Chingwe returned, his granddaughter said, "Grandfather, come, sit beside me and have some of these mushrooms. We have plenty so take as many as you want."

She had removed the skillet from the fire and had it setting beside her to cool. The boys came over and sat down with her and her Grandfather. She placed the skillet on the ground in front of them and they took turns picking mushrooms out of the fat and popping them into their mouths.

When they finished the mushrooms, Dark Sky removed the squirrel from the fire and carried it over to his Grandfather. The old man cut the squirrel up and divided it evenly.

"This was a good meal." The old man said. "Thank you, Dark Sky, for providing us with that squirrel. And thank you Blue Feather for finding and preparing those delicious mushrooms. You are almost as good a cook as your mother."

As he sat there he felt pressure building in his lower stomach. He squirmed and broke wind. The children began laughing and he held up his hand.

"Hush children, hush, the spirits are trying to tell us something!"

He held up his hands towards the sky and said, "Speak old toothless one!"

He let go another round of gas and started laughing. The children rolled on the ground laughing so hard.

The sun was on its downward slide and the old man said, "Go and fetch some more wood for the fire and we will sit and talk for a while before we go to sleep."

The children scurried off into the woods in different directions to relieve themselves and gather some more firewood. The old man went off by himself and as he stood there, he looked up into the sky at the dark clouds on the western horizon. "It looks like the rain will be here before morning." He thought, "I hope it will not bring strong winds."

He glanced towards the shelter. "It looks as though it will be able to stand a strong storm and keep us dry." He walked over and inspected the hides and tightened the strips of rawhide used to tie them down. He looked over the trench the boys had dug around the edge to channel any running water away from the shelter. Satisfied, he walked over to the fire and sat down.

The children brought their wood in and placed it in a pile next to the fire. They sat down and begged their Grandfather to tell them of his childhood and his life here at this place.

I will begin by telling you of my father James Letart Jr. Cahiktodo was his Shawnee name. He was born in that cabin we visited today. My mother told me that he was very intelligent. By the time he was ten summers old, he could speak fluently in Algonquin, French, English as well as the language of the Iroquois. He learned this from his father and the people who came to the cabin to trade.

Although he was half French and half Shawnee, he spent more time with the Indians than with the whites who frequented the trading post. He had the dark complexion and hair of an Indian but his eyes were as blue as the summer sky.

As a small boy, he would row his canoe over to the village and spend most of his time playing with the boys there and learning the Shawnee and Delaware ways of life. This proved invaluable to his father's trading business and he hoped later on in life Cahiktodo would be one of his best traders.

Cahiktodo excelled in all the games and events that occurred in Little Buck Town and was a friend to everyone there. He had no enemies and later in his life he became the village Chief there.

He was known for his ability to think and reason. He would seek to prevent discord but would not turn his back on a fight if needed. His reputation as a warrior was well known.

When but a young man, he fell in love and took as his wife my mother, Chihopekelis, Bluebird. She told me she kept her eye on him since he first visited the village as a small boy and she a small girl. She knew in her heart that one day he and her would be together.

When she was a little girl, she used to try to get his attention, but he would just ignore her. She would watch for his canoe and rush down to the river so she would be standing there on the bank when he beached. She would always greet him with a smile, but most of the time all she got in return was a nod of his head as he hurried to meet with his friends at the village.

She even made gifts for him. With the help of her mother she once made him a pair of moccasins from the soft hide of a doe. When she handed them to him, he just grunted and gave her a fang from the mouth of a Bobcat as if trading with her. She kept that tooth and wore it on a beaded necklace for the rest of her life.

It was not until she started to become a woman that Cahiktodo began to take a sincere interest in her. She was usually the first person he saw when he rowed across the river to Little Buck Town because she always watched for him and when she saw him coming she would rush down to the river to be there when he arrived.

One morning when my father was about fourteen summers, he rowed across the river from the cabin to visit his friends in the village. Bluebird was sitting on the bank as usual. She was running a comb through her long black hair. Cahiktodo had never seen her before without her hair being in tied in braids along side of her head. He beached his canoe and walked over to her.

"A Cherokee warrior would be proud to have that hair hanging from his scalp belt Bluebird. You should take care coming down here by yourself."

"I wasn't by myself, Cahiktodo, I saw you leave the other shore before I came down here. I knew I would be safe with you around."

"A good warrior would have slit your throat, took your scalp and be gone before I could have gotten halfway across."

She looked over at him and their eyes locked. He was lost in her beauty and didn't notice when she reached down and picked up a tomahawk she had hidden beneath her skirt. She suddenly jerked and brought it around striking him not too gently in the side of his head with the flat edge.

"EEE YOW!" he cried as he grabbed the side of his head and rubbed it vigorously with his hand. "Why did you do that Bluebird?"

"See," she said, "I was prepared. Had you been a Cherokee, I would have buried the hawk in your skull and taken your scalp. Don't think, Cahiktodo, that just because I am a woman, I cannot defend myself."

Rubbing the side of his head, Cahiktodo laughed and said, "If I can get permission from my father, I will be permitted to join the next raiding party to Cherokee country. I will warn the whole Cherokee nation to stay away from this place or they will risk losing their sons to the great, long haired warrior Bluebird."

They both laughed at his remark.

Gazing into her eyes again, he said, "Bluebird, why did your parents give you that name?"

"On the morning I was born, my father stepped out of the wigwam and a bluebird landed at his feet and began hopping around looking for something to eat. He was not afraid of my father standing there. My father went back inside the wigwam and told my mother about it so they named me Bluebird right then and there."

Cahiktodo stood up and held out his hand. "Come Bluebird, let's you and I take a walk down the river bank."

"Your friends are waiting for you Cahiktodo, they will be angry if you do not go to them."

"Let them be angry, they will soon get over it. There is nothing today that we cannot do tomorrow and besides, they are not half as beautiful as you are. Come let's walk."

As they strolled along side by side, he told her of his father and the fur trade he had. He told her of his desire to be a warrior, but his father was trying to persuade him to join him in his trading business. He was torn between his loyalty to his father and his desire to be a Shawnee warrior.

"I know your father, Bluebird. He is a great Lenape warrior. His name alone strikes fear into the hearts of our enemies the Cherokee. It is like him that I want to be. He has the respect of all the people in the Delaware and Shawnee nations. But my father is determined that I should become a trader like himself. He has told me that he does not want me to ever forget that I am half French."

He stopped and held out his left arm towards Bluebird.

"Look. When I was just a small boy, he had a Frenchman put this tattoo on my arm."

With his palm facing upward, he showed the tattoo to Bluebird.

"What is that?" Bluebird asked, "It looks so strange."

"It is the letters of my French name LETART. My father said he had it put there to remind me always that I am half French and that I carry the name of his ancestors."

"Maybe I should not tell you this Cahiktodo, because you must make up your own mind on the path of life you are to follow, but I have heard my father speak of you often. He said that you are a better marksman with the bow and rifle than most of the warriors who accompanied him on the last raid to the Cherokee country. He spoke of how you seem to stand out among your friends and take charge of activities. He has said that some day you will be a great warrior and perhaps even a chief, even though you are half French."

"To hear that your father has said these things makes my heart feel like it is a running deer. I am very pleased that your father has noticed me and said these things about me. If I am permitted to go on the next raid, I will show everyone that I can be a great warrior! Maybe not as great as your father, but I will do my best to please him and my father also. Perhaps my father will see then that my heart really lies with my brothers, the Shawnee and Lenape. Trading is a white man's business."

"Your father is Shawnee."

"That is true Bluebird, but he was adopted, but his blood is still French. He is loyal to the tribe, but still, he has the white mans' way of doing things. I love my father and am proud of the way he lives, but I have not yet figured out if I could live that way."

"I am sure, whichever path you choose to walk; it will be the right one," said Bluebird, "And no one, not even my father, will judge you on your decision."

"Cahiktodo! There you are! We have been searching for you!"

The voice came from above the river bank. It was his friend Tahkox, the Turtle. He made a lot of noise coming down the top of the hill through the brush.

"My grandfather wants a turkey for his supper tonight. Me and my brother were hoping you would help us get one for him."

He looked surprised when he noticed Bluebird standing beside Cahiktodo. "Why are you with her?"

"We were just talking, Turtle. Where is your brother?"

"He's is searching for you near the creek. Come, let's go to him."

"You go ahead Turtle. I will meet you there after I walk Bluebird to the village."

"Can she not walk by herself? She's a big girl."

"Just go, Turtle! I will join you soon!"

"Women!" Turtle muttered under his breath as he made his way back up the hill.

"Turtle seemed angry that you were with me," said Bluebird. "I don't think he likes me."

"He likes you well enough" replied Cahiktodo as he took her hands in his. "Bluebird, may I come and visit you from time to time?"

"You will have to ask permission from my father, but I am sure he would give it willingly."

"Before I go back across the river, I will speak to him and ask for his permission. I enjoyed talking with you today, Bluebird. I don't know why we never spoke much before."

"It wasn't because of me," said Bluebird. "I have been waiting for you to notice me for a long, long time. We'd better head back, your friends are impatient."

As they turned to walk back toward the village, Cahiktodo reached down and took Bluebird's hand in his own and at that moment, a bond developed between the two that would last their entire lives.

Chingwe paused in his story telling and looked at his grandchildren. They were looking at him with eyes wide in anticipation.

"Tell us more Grandfather... did Cahiktodo get to go to the Cherokee country?"

"Go and fetch my pipe Squirrel and I will tell you a little more before we lay down to sleep."

Squirrel hurriedly ran to the shelter and found his Grandfather's pipe and tobacco pouch. As his Grandfather filled the pipe with tobacco, Blue Feather held a stick in the fire. When it ignited she handed it to her Grandfather who then lit his pipe. As he puffed, the blue smoke swirled about his head.

From a long way off, the rumble of distant thunder could be heard but the sky above them was clear and filled with thousands of stars. There was no wind so to speak, just the occasional zephyr of cool late spring air.

In the flickering glow of the firelight, Chingwe continued his story.

My father did get permission to go on that raid, but only after Bluebird's father went across the river and assured my Grandfather that he would personally look after Cahiktodo and would do everything possible to assure his safety.

Cahiktodo did well on his first raid. Although he did not return with any Cherokee scalps, he managed to capture three Cherokee horses all by himself. He took them right under the nose of a Cherokee boy who was supposed to be watching the village herd. Cahiktodo did not kill him because, he said afterward, "He looked so much like my friend Turtle that I could not make myself do it. I just snuck up on him and struck him with the flat side of my tomahawk, knocking him out."

He gave one of the horses to his father, one to Bluebird's father and kept the other one for himself.

He witnessed the death of a friend for the first time. One of their party was captured and killed by the Cherokee. His scalped, lifeless body was found by Cahiktodo and I believe the effect of that and witnessing the killing of several Cherokee may have changed his outlook on being a warrior.

Oh, he was noted as a brave and fearless warrior and did bring home some scalps in other raids, but he also gained the reputation of being merciful. Many times, he allowed his adversary to live without taking a scalp.

He once told me it seemed to him that killing of animals for food, clothing and shelter was acceptable, but taking the life of another human being was repugnant to him and he attempted to avoid having to do so unless he had to save his own life or that of a friend. Some looked upon this as weakness, but others saw it as strength.

When Cahiktodo was about nineteen summers, he took my mother as his wife. He had courted Bluebird over the years and was accepted into her mother's family with open arms.

Cahiktodo and Bluebird took part in the wedding dance one spring night with several other couples. They pledged themselves to each other for eternity as they embraced. My mother told me it was one of the happiest moments in her life.

He taught her to speak in French and English just as his father taught him.

She was just about the same age as Cahiktodo and her beauty was well known in the area. Before the wedding dance, a French courier who worked for my Grandfather had attempted to court her but he was rebuffed.

A Delaware warrior from the village of Old Town once came to our village and he also attempted to court her. He too was rebuffed by Bluebird, but he kept hanging around trying to gain her attention. My father met him in the woods one day, near our village and with some "not too gentle" persuasion convinced the Delaware to leave and go back to his home.

Chapter Three

Pausing only long enough to light his pipe, Chingwe continued his story:

Soon after I was born, there was a great war between the British and the French. They both wanted control of the lands west of the Appalachians and the trade with the Indian nations living there. The British wanted more than trade though. They also wanted to take our land and open it up for settlement by their colonists.

Most of the Indian nations sided with the French who were noted for conducting their trading business more fairly with the Indians and had no intentions of sending settlers to occupy the land. These nations included the Shawnee, Lenape, Huron, Pottawatomie, Ottawa, Mississauga and Mingo.

Although my grandfather was a Frenchman by birth and a Shawnee by adoption, his loyalties were with his employer, the British West Jersey Trading Company but not necessarily with the British Government. Unlike the Ohio Company who had also set up trading posts west of the Appalachians, the West Jersey Trading Company had no intentions of trading for land to be opened for settlement by the British Colonists. He and the men who worked for him remained neutral throughout the war.

My father was loyal to the Shawnee people and when the war chiefs called for their warriors to strike the British he went with them. Grandfather opposed this but as Cahiktodo was now a man, there was little he could do but try to talk him out of fighting.

My father went east to join with the Shawnee and Lenape who were allied with the French. The French had built a fort in Pennsylvania where the Ohio River begins and had named it Fort Duquesne. It was a very important place to have a fort. It gave the forces holding it control of a large area. The British wanted it badly.

About a year after the French had built the fort, British General Braddock and about 2000 men attempted to capture it. Braddock was a fool! He considered the Indian Nations that had allied with the French to be inferior to his fighting force. He didn't trust any Indian and wouldn't even listen to the reports brought to him from the Oneida scouts of his own army.

He attempted to haul huge cannons through the wilderness from his Fort Cumberland in Maryland to Fort Duquesne. Along with his fighting force he was accompanied by train of supply wagons, over two hundred and fifty sutlers and women. This greatly slowed down his advance to the fort.

My father told me what happened. The French and their allies were waiting for Braddock. They had intended to set up an ambush at the crossing on the Monongahela River, but they waited too long and the British forded the great river unmolested.

The French commander then sent out a force of about 900 of their soldiers and warriors to confront the approaching enemy. My father was among them and he told me that the British had not even sent out flankers upon their approach to the fort. They came walking down the trail casually, some not even carrying their muskets.

The French and Indians had positioned themselves in the woods on both sides of the little valley about eight or ten miles from the fort. They were to wait in hiding until the head of the British column reached the last man set in the ambush but as the head of the column neared this position, a group of Ottawa became impatient and attacked the rear of the column.

Their screams and shots caused the soldiers at the head of the column to stop and turn around to see what was happening in the rear. At that time, a French officer jumped up and gave the command to fire.

The woods on both sides seemed to explode and many British soldiers fell dead or wounded on that first volley. As the French and Indians reloaded and fired at will, billowing white smoke from their muskets filled the air along with the war cries of the attackers, the screaming of the wounded and the return fire of a few of the soldiers in the column.

These screams of the wounded and war cries of their unseen attackers caused great fear and confusion among the British. Some were firing wildly at the woods, their shots doing no harm to the ambushers.

General Braddock appeared on horseback and was attempting to rally his men to form ranks and return fire in volleys. He refused to allow his rangers and militiamen to enter the woods to take the fight there.

Braddock was a very foolish man but he was also a very brave man. My father said he had four horses shot out from under him during this fight and was wounded badly while attempting to mount a fifth.

He could not get the men to form adequate ranks. Individual warriors began to emerge from the woods and rush screaming and yelling to attack the British soldiers as they huddled in masses.

The soldiers were all trying to gain the safety of the center of the masses and very few were even firing their muskets. Terror and confusion was their main response to the attack. Some were hacked to death by tomahawks as they lay on the ground, whimpering in fright, not even attempting to put up a fight.

With General Braddock wounded and unable to command, some of his officers tried to rally the men, but they too were soon cut down. Amongst the blood and gore, total fear took hold of the few remaining men who were not wounded and they threw down their arms and stripped themselves of anything that could hold them back and began to run back down the trail.

Some attempted to help the wounded escape but most ran like wild men to escape the onslaught of the enemy. As these retreating men collided with the advancing supply train, their fear and confusion caused the women and sutlers to react the same way. Drivers bailed off their wagons and took flight on foot. Women screamed as the pursuing attackers caught them and clubbed them to death with their tomahawks. The whole army was now a mass of bloody, fear choked men and women each trying to run away from the most terrible event they had ever experienced.

Had it not been for their officer Washington the victory would have been complete. All of the British soldiers would have been slain.

Once across the Monongahela, Washington managed to form the soldiers into an organized retreat with formations adequately formed to protect the rear and flanks. They solemnly made their way back to their Fort Cumberland. Along the way, General Braddock died of his wounds and was buried underneath the trail.

This, my father said, he learned from prisoners taken well after the fight.

My father said the British lost over 450 men killed and over 500 wounded in that fight. The French and Indian force had only 28 men killed.

A great many of the British were captured and taken to Fort Duquesne. Some of these captives were tortured and burned at the stake there. This deeply upset my father who was against such things and he told those with him that if any of them ever partook in such a practice, he would have nothing else to do with them.

My father told me that after they had fought Braddock's army, they were successful in driving some of the colonists back towards the east coast. However the British were determined to push back and force the French out of the area.

The King of England appointed a new British Commander named Forbes and he gathered over 6000 men from Pennsylvania and Virginia along with his regulars. He led this new force west to again attack the French and attempt to capture Fort Duquesne.

As this new force neared Fort Duquesne, General Forbes sent out a force of about 750 men under the command of a Major Grant to scout out the fort's defenses. As this advance scouting force approached the fort, Grant foolishly ordered the pipers who were accompanying him to play! The sound of the bagpipes alerted Captain de Lignery, who was now commanding the fort that the British were approaching. He sent out a force around 500 men to attack them.

My father and his friends were part of this attacking force. They surrounded the British and opened fire with their muskets. At the first volley nearly a hundred of the British threw down their weapons without firing a shot and deserted. It didn't take long for the panic to spread and soon the whole column was in full retreat through a gap in the French and Indian lines. The British lost a lot of men. Grant and eighteen others were captured and taken to the fort.

Although the French and Indians were victorious in this fight Captain de Lignery knew that the French would not be able to hold out against the rest of the British force now approaching the fort. It was decided to abandon it. Before they left, the French garrison set fire to the fort and departed under the cover of darkness.

When the British arrived at the smoldering remains of the fort they found the Indians had killed the recently captured soldiers and had impaled their heads on sharp stakes on top of the fort's walls.

My father was disgusted with the French for allowing their Indian allies to do such a thing and he and his friends returned to Little Buck Town. They would fight no more in this war.

They were convinced that it would be just a matter of time before the British were victorious over the French. The Lenape and the Shawnee along with many others signed a treaty with the British giving up their alliance with the French. The British promised that after the war, they would remove all their military out of the area. Of course they lied. They rebuilt the fort and named it Fort Pitt. It is there still to this day.

"Children, I must go and relieve myself." Chingwe said as he slowly got to his feet and started towards the woods. The children jumped up and went their separate ways to do the same.

Chapter Four

Once they all returned and sat down, Chingwe continued his story.

Soon after he returned from this war, my father moved from the area of grandfather's cabin across the river to Little Buck Town. He built a wigwam of bark and wood on the bank along the river just below the falls. He maintained his loyalty to my grandfather and my grandfather was determined that his son would take over his trading business when he passed on.

One of the most important parts of my grandfather's business was to send the furs he received in trade to the city of Philadelphia. It was a long and arduous journey upriver on canoes to the Allegheny, then to Fort Pitt where the furs were to be loaded into carts and taken overland to Philadelphia.

My grandfather hired couriers to take the furs to Philadelphia and return with supplies and sundries to trade with the Indians for more furs. At the urging of my grandfather, Cahiktodo and Bluebird were to travel to Philadelphia with the furs. He wanted them to meet the people of the West Jersey Trading Company. He hoped their influence would help Cahiktodo make up his mind to stay in the trading business. I would stay with my grandfather.

There were about fifteen or twenty canoes laden with furs, each with two people to row upriver against the current. It was the first time that Bluebird had left the peaceful tranquility of the village and the surrounding area. She was a little excited and a little afraid at the same time. She had heard stories of the soldiers at Fort Pitt and the people of the city of Philadelphia but had never imagined she would ever visit those places.

My grandfather had written a letter of introduction to the fur company in Philadelphia and gave it to Cahiktodo to present to the company officials upon arrival there. He also gave him a list of needed supplies and trade goods.

Along with this flotilla of fur laden canoes were two large war canoes, each manned by five men armed with muskets. These men were both French couriers and warriors from the village hired by my grandfather to protect his furs. One of these canoes was commanded by Jean Lebeau who was the Head Courier. He would lead the flotilla upriver. The other was commanded by Christopher Burkey, an Englishman who had worked for my grandfather for years and was greatly trusted by him. His would follow the flotilla to protect their rear.

At the bow of both of these war canoes were mounted a small brass cannon. It was the responsibility of these two canoes to protect the fur laden canoes from attack by river pirates or other hostiles intent on capturing the furs for trade themselves.

Before the flotilla started their journey, my grandfather pulled my father aside and said to him, "Cahiktodo, everyone on this journey, including my brother's men, know that you are my son and that I have placed you in command. I know you are capable of making sound decisions on your own, but I strongly advise that you always seek counsel with Jean and Christopher and listen to their advice. They have both made this journey several times. They know what they are doing and what to expect. Now go my son, make haste, but be cautious and alert. There are many dangers between here and Philadelphia."

The first few days of their journey upriver were uneventful except for one instance where one of the fur laden canoes overturned while navigating through the Rapids. No lives were lost and the furs were recovered.

They stopped at the trading post of my grandfather's brother Jacques and he added another ten or so canoes full of furs to accompany the flotilla to Pennsylvania.

A day after they left the trading post of Jacques, they came upon an area the Frenchmen called "The Palisades". For a stretch of about a mile or so the hillsides seemed to drop straight down into the river. There are half submerged boulders strewn all over the river there. Bluebird thought this was the most beautiful place she had ever seen.

"Look!" she shouted to Cahiktodo as she pointed to the top of one of the high hills. "Aren't they beautiful?"

As Cahiktodo looked up he saw a large herd of Whitetail Deer led by a huge buck with a full head of antlers. They were walking along the ridgeline, high above the river.

"Yes, they are beautiful. One of them would make fine eating if we could just get to them."

Burkey's large canoe surged past Cahiktodo's canoe and as it passed by one of the Frenchman shouted, "We are going on up ahead and once we are out of the Palisades, we will find a place to make camp. We will also get us some fresh meat for supper tonight."

About a mile or two after the flotilla left the Palisades area they came upon the beached canoe of the men who had gone ahead. Cahiktodo heard two shots ring out in the forest as he beached their canoe along side the big one. "Sounds like we will have venison tonight." he said as struggled to pull the canoe up from the water.

After all the canoes were beached and guards were posted the group began setting up a camp. The sky was clear but some chose to make shelters anyway while others decided to just sleep on the breast of Mother Earth without shelter. Fires were built and after the hunters returned with two fat does they gutted the deer and divided the meat equally. Soon the aroma of roasting venison filled the air.

They decided to stay at this place for a couple of days to rest from their labors rowing upriver through the rapids and the Palisades. The river current was still strong but no way near the strength of the Rapids. The upriver trip from here would be much easier. A hunting party was selected to go out in the morning in search of more fresh meat.

As the sun was just beginning to settle over the hilltops, a huge swirling black cloud appeared in the heavens above the ridgeline across the river. The men stopped what they were doing and stood there staring at the approaching mass in the sky. Bluebird was frightened as the cloud grew in size and began moving towards the encampment.

"What is that?" she cried as she covered her ears.

A sound like the rushing winds of a surging storm filled the air. It was like the noise of a million flapping wings mixed with gurgling and cooing sounds that became louder and louder as the cloud approached.

In fact it was wings. As the leading edge of the cloud reached the camp it proved to be a large flock of Passenger Pigeons. The flock seemed to reach from horizon to horizon. Small globs of pigeon dung began dropping from the sky like snowflakes. It got progressively darker as the huge number of birds seemed to block out the waning sun.

The men began firing their muskets into that mass in the sky, not aiming, just holding up their muskets and pulling the trigger. They would then reload and fire again and again. Birds began dropping from the sky and soon the camp was littered with dead and dying birds. Sometimes a single shot would bring down three or four birds. It took almost an hour for the flock to pass and by that time the group had enough pigeons to provide food for several days.

Cahiktodo and Bluebird were amazed. Neither had ever seen such a sight before. As they helped gather the birds Cahiktodo said he had often heard of such things from the people who traded with his father, but had never imagined the magnitude of these flocks.

One day as the flotilla made its way around a small bend in the river they came upon three canoes heading downriver on the opposite side. Each canoe held three frontiersmen dressed in greasy buckskin. The frontiersmen pulled their canoes together and were setting there intently watching the flotilla.

Concerned by the potential danger of attack, Jean ordered the canoes to bunch together. The men in the war canoes checked their firearms and kept a close eye on the frontiersmen.

Suddenly the three canoes broke up and the frontiersmen began paddling rapidly across the river towards the flotilla.

The war canoe in the rear of the flotilla increased its speed and changed course towards the approaching frontiersmen. In the bow, Burkey shouted for the frontiersmen to turn back. They did not reply. They kept paddling boldly towards the flotilla. Burkey shouted another warning which went unheeded and unanswered.

Apparently the frontiersmen didn't notice the small cannon mounted in the bow of the big canoe. It was loaded with small lead balls, some broken chain links and even a few rocks. Burkey lit the fuse. There was loud boom and a cloud of smoke as the cannon went off sending a spray of hot metal across the bows of the approaching canoes.

A small piece of shrapnel caught one of the frontiersmen in the shoulder, knocking him over the side of his canoe. Sputtering and cursing he struggled to climb back in as his friends frantically paddled to change their course. Once back in his canoe the wounded frontiersman raised his fist and shouted a curse at Burkey but they offered no return fire and went back to their downriver course.

"We will have to post extra guards from now on," Burkey said to Lebeau who had brought his war canoe back to help. "They may come back and try to catch us unawares."

Daniel Greathouse, a big burly frontiersman sat in the middle of the lead canoe clutching his wounded shoulder.

"Grills, beach us over there and get this damn thing out of my shoulder, it's burning like hell's fire. Those sons of bitches are going to pay for this."

Grills beached the canoe and helped Greathouse remove his shirt. "It's just a small piece" said Grills, "Just under the skin."

He used his knife to pry a small piece of metal from Daniel's shoulder. We ain't got nothin' to bandage it with."

"Never mind that Grills! Just get the damned bleedin' to stop!"

Grills used Daniel's greasy buckskin shirt to help staunch the bleeding. Once he got it stopped he dunked the shirt in the river water to wash out the blood.

"Let's go up on the bank and build a fire to dry out your clothes."

Grills soon had a good fire going and using stakes stuck in the ground, he draped Daniel's clothes near it to hasten their drying.

Sitting there wrapped in a trader's blanket, Greathouse said. "That was a trader's flotilla. They'll be coming back downriver someday soon, loaded with supplies and trade goods. We'll set up a surprise for 'em. Maybe we'll be startin' up a little tradin' business of our own."

Chapter Five

On the point of land where the Allegheny and Monongahela Rivers meet to form the Great Ohio, stands Fort Pitt. It was once named Fort Duquesne and was originally built by the French. It was now occupied by British troops and had been renamed Fort Pitt in honor of William Pitt, the British Prime Minister. The conqueror was General John Forbes. The present commander is General John Stanwix.

Surrounding the fort are numerous trader's cabins, weigwas, wigwam s and bark houses. There are great gardens and fields of corn guarded by the red coated soldiers of His Majesty's army.

As the flotilla neared the beach in front of the fort, Bluebird was in awe of the sight. The main gates of the fort were open and there were people milling about. There were groups coming and going, in and out of the gate.

There were formations of red coated soldiers marching about in drill. Frontiersmen and traders clad in dark oily buckskin mixed with Indians of many different nations, Shawnee, Lenape, Wyandot, Conestoga etc. There were even a group of Mohawks from the Six Nation Confederation of Iroquois.

Some Indians were dressed in buckskins as were the frontiersman, some in breech cloths and blankets. Almost all of the men carried rifles. The air was filled with a cacophony of sound as the different dialects being spoken mixed with the busy sounds of people working and carrying out their everyday chores.

As they floated near the shore they saw a frontiersman on his knees washing his face in the river. He stood up and shouted, "Hello there. Where you comin' from?"

Cahiktodo jumped at the chance the chance to speak in English. “From Letart’s trading post, down the river in the Great Bend.”

“Welcome, my name’s Girty...Simon Girty.” He reached down and was helping Cahiktodo beach the canoe.

“I am Cahiktodo or James Letart Jr. Son of James Letart the trader and this is my woman Bluebird.”

“Hello there Bluebird,” Simon said as he reached out his hand to help her out of the canoe. “My oh my James, you sure have a pretty wife. You’d better keep an eye on her. You can’t trust those mangy soldiers from the fort. They could care less if she’s a married woman or not!”

“Are you hungry? Got me some fresh venison over there I would be glad to share with you. I’d like to hear about the country downriver. What do you say? Care to join me for supper?”

Cahiktodo took an immediate liking to this friendly, young frontiersman and agreed to eat with him that evening.

“What happened to your head?” he asked as he noticed blood flowing slightly from behind the frontiersman’s ear.

“Oh, I got myself in a tussle with a couple of those bastard red coats. They think they’re so much better than everyone else. I caught a couple of them cheating an old Conestoga, who is a friend of mine, out of some tobacco he had. When I confronted them about it they jumped me. I knocked one of them senseless after he caught me upside the head with his rifle butt and had my knife at the other one’s throat when my friend Butler, Simon Butler, grabbed me and pulled me off him. If it hadn’t been for Butler, I probably would have killed that no good son-of-a-bitch!”

"My advice to you James is this, you and your men stay clear of them red coats if you can and never, ever deal with more than one or two of them at a time. I reckon some of your men know how those red coats feel about Frenchies. So make sure those in your group stay well clear of them."

"Thank you for your advice Mr. Girty."

"Call me Simon."

"Thank you for your advice Simon. And please, call me by my Shawnee name, Cahiktodo. My men and I have had experience in dealing with men of all ilk but we will watch our backs around here."

Jean Lebeau and Christopher Burkey came up to them and Lebeau said. "Come Cahiktodo, we must go see if the wagons are here."

Cahiktodo introduced the two to Simon and Simon said, "They are here, four of 'em. They came in about three days ago. Come on, I'll take you to where they're at. They're on the back side of the fort."

Simon led the four towards the rear of the fort. As they walked along he said to Cahiktodo, "There's one more thing you need to be aware of. Wetzel's in the area, you have to be very careful and alert when he is around."

"Who is this Wetzel?" Cahiktodo asked.

"Lewis Wetzel is his full name but some call him The Death Wind. He is plumb crazy I tell you, and he hates Indians. All Indians, it don't matter to him whether they be man, woman or child or what nation they be. They are all fair game to him. He is driven to kill all the Indians he can."

"He ain't supposed to be near the fort because General Stanwix banished him from the area, but him and his brother snuck in the other night to get some rum. They ended up killing and scalping a couple Wyandots. That scream of his brought the whole fort to arms and Forbes sent out soldiers to capture him. Of course they didn't catch him. He's a better woodsman than anybody in the whole world. Once he's in the woods he just disappears!"

"Why does he hate the Indians so?" Bluebird asked.

"I'm not sure but I heard that when he was just a lad, a party of Shawnee attacked his father's cabin over in Virginia and did some pretty bad things. He and his brother were captured but managed to escape. It must have done something to his mind. Whenever he makes a kill, he lets go with this God-awful scream. I heard it before. It sounds worse than a wounded panther and three times as loud. It'll make the hair on the back of your neck stand up. That's why some call him The Death Wind. When you hear that sound, you know some poor soul has just lost his life."

"Girty!"

A British Sergeant and two privates walked up to the party. "General Stanwix wants to see you. He is going to parley with the Mohawks and wants you to interpret."

He paused and looked over Bluebird from head to foot. She averted her eyes from him.

"Where did you get this pretty little bitch? Clean her up and sneak her into my quarters tonight and I'll give you a pint of rum."

In that instant, Cahiktodo, Lebeau and Burkey pulled their tomahawks from their belt. The red coats took an engarde position and Cahiktodo was in the process of lunging towards the offending sergeant.

Simon managed to grab Cahiktodo and held him tightly as he struggled to get to his adversary. Sergeant Stewart pulled a pistol from his belt and leveled it at Cahiktodo.

“Touch a hair on her head,” shouted Cahiktodo, “And I guarantee your hair will be hanging on my belt!”

“My, my, Girty,” smirked the Sergeant, “You must be coming up in the world! The friends you are keeping now seem to be more educated than the ignorant animals you usually hang around with. This savage speaks better English than you!”

Girty replied, “The only ignorant animals I see around here is you, you pompous bastard, and if you don’t leave right now, I’m gonna turn my friend here loose on ya!”

Eyeing Burkey and Lebeau, Sergeant Stewart returned the pistol to his belt. He barked an order for the two privates to follow him and walked away in a huff back towards the front of the fort.

“Now you know what I was talking about.” Simon said, “It makes you kinda wish the French had won the war.”

Simon pointed to a campsite on the edge of the woods and said, “There’s where your wagons are. I had better go see what Stanwix wants. I’ll also tell him of the incident we just had. I doubt if he’ll do anything about it though...he’s sometimes just as bad as the others.”

I’ll see you all tonight over at my camp just downriver from where you beached your canoes. Burkey, you and Lebeau are welcome to come along too if you’d like.”

They shook hands and Simon turned to go to the fort.

As the group neared the wagons one of the drivers came up and asked Burkey, “Are you Letort?”

“No, not I, I’m Christopher Burkey, this gentleman is Jean Lebeau, head courier.”

Putting his hand on Cahiktodo’s shoulder he said, “And this here is James Letart Junior, the son of

James Letart. And this is his wife Chihopekelis or Bluebird."

The driver looked at Cahiktodo and muttered in surprise, "Why he's an Indian!"

Cahiktodo said, "My father is adopted Shawnee, my mother is Shawnee, I am Shawnee but I am also half French. My father sent me here in his place to represent him."

"I beg your pardon James. I apologize for being such a dolt. My name is Henry, Henry Weber, Head Wagoner and I am pleased to meet you."

They shook hands all around and Henry said, "Let's round up the other drivers, fetch the wagons and go down to the river to load up."

Once the wagons were loaded and all the canoes pulled up on the shore, Jean and Christopher selected some of their best men to stay and guard the canoes and supplies. The rest would travel along as guards with the wagons to Philadelphia. They pulled the wagons back to the campsite at the rear of the fort.

"We will leave here in the morning for Philadelphia. It is a long and arduous journey so get plenty of rest tonight. You may dine with us if you wish."

"Thank you for your invitation Henry", replied Cahiktodo, "but we have already accepted an offer of dinner from Mr. Girty. We will stay at his camp tonight and will be here early in the morning to begin our journey. "

The four made their way to Girty's camp and were greeted with a smile and handshakes all around. "Got a fine meal cookin'. Had that deer roastin' all day and I traded for some okeepenauk and got 'em bakin' in the coals."

"What is okeepenauk?" Burkey asked.

“Wild taters...sort of like sweet taters only better. I know most people don’t eat a big supper, but when you’re hungry, you’re hungry. Well have plenty left over for breakfast in the morning. C’mon, let’s get started on it.”

Everyone helped themselves to the venison and each one pulled one of the okeepenauk from the coals.

“I have a little salt if anyone wants some.” Simon said. He tossed the bag over to Burkey who reached in and took a little salt in his fingers. He sprinkled it over his meat and his okeepenauk.

“This tater tastes pretty good Simon. A little salt helps it though.”

As they ate, the guests told Simon of their journey.

After they had all eaten their fill, Simon lit a pipe and passed it around. “Tell me Bluebird, what’s it like back where you’re from?”

“It is a beautiful place. We live in a small village called Quenolapay Ohtenatit just below the falls on the Spaylawetheepi. The land there is very rich and we grow corn, squash, pumpkins and sunflower. The river teems with fish of all kinds and the woods around us are full of deer, bear, buffalo, turkey, squirrels and other animals that provide us meat.”

“In the winter, the hills behind us and across the river are sometimes white with snow. Sometimes, the river freezes over and you can actually walk across it, except below the falls, which never freezes.”

“In the springtime, the hills turn green and the valley is filled with flowers of every kind. Their perfume drifts through the air which sometimes seems filled with every kind of bird there is. Blue ones, yellow ones, red ones...all with their own song.

“The hills are most beautiful in the fall. The trees in some places seem to be afire. The hills are painted in colors of gold, red, yellow and green. The cool fall breezes send their falling leaves flying through the air. As children we use to gather them up into big piles and run and jump into them. It was so much fun."

"My favorite thing about our home is the falls. The sound of the water rushing over it creates a soothing sound that quiets the soul and helps you sleep during those hot summer nights."

"That is also my favorite thing about our village" said Cahiktodo. In my lifetime we have always known peace there. In the past, the Cherokee have sent warriors into our area to raid and they have attacked and stolen horses from the village of Old Town, which is just north east of us, but they have never raided Quenolapay Ohtenatit."

"Why is it named Little Buck Town, my friend? Girty asked.

"I do not know, Simon. It has always been called that. Perhaps because of the deer that abound in that area. Tell us about yourself Simon. Where are you from?"

"I was born east of here and about four years ago Delaware warriors attacked my family. Me and my brothers were captured. I was traded to and adopted by the Seneca while my brother James was adopted by the Shawnee...my brother George by the Delaware."

"I'm here now hired on as an interpreter for the British. I thoroughly dislike and distrust them, but a man has to make a living."

"I am close though, to giving up trying to make it as a white man and going back to my Seneca brothers. I can see what these British are up to. They and the French are each just about as bad as the other, maybe the British a little worse. They both want to take over the whole country and rule over all the Nations. They want to open up the Indian lands for settlement by their own people!"

"It's sickening the way the British lie to the Nations and unbelievable that the nations tend to believe them. To most of them, any Indian is nothing more than an animal in the way of their so called civilization."

Cahiktodo said, "There are very few white men near our village, except for Burkey and Lebeau here. My father, James Letart, is French by birth but Shawnee by adoption. We see a few white traders now and then who come to visit my father. We have had no problems with whites so far."

"Mark my word Cahiktodo, you will, and soon I reckon. The British know about the rich lands of the Ohio Country. They'll soon be trying to wrest the lands from the people living there, just like they're doing here in the east now. It's just a matter of time."

"Cahiktodo stood and said, "Simon, it has been a real pleasure talking to you. I hope your life turns out well. We must retire now as we are rising early in the morning to begin our journey to Philadelphia to turn in our furs and pick up supplies for my father."

"I want you to know that you will always be welcome at our village and my father's trading post. I hope someday you can come visit us. I will not forget your hospitality here."

"Thank you Cahiktodo, I just might come visit you and Bluebird at your village some day. It would be nice to get away from the hustle and bustle of this place...yes...I just might take you up on that."

Chapter Six

Chingwe paused in his story telling to look at the children. Blue Feather and Dark Sky were sitting there with eyes wide, listening to his words. Gray Squirrel had fallen asleep next to the fire.

Clouds had drifted overhead and a shower was moving in. It had begun to sprinkle. Chingwe smiled as a rain drop fell and struck Gray Squirrel between his eyes, splattering across his face. The shock of the cold rain drop caused him to awaken and jerk up into a sitting position. He rubbed his eyes.

"Come children let's go to the shelter."

They hurriedly picked up the items they had with them around the fire and scurried to the shelter. They entered and lay down upon the soft bed they made of grasses they collected from the banks of the river. Chingwe covered them with a large black bear skin they had brought with them. He lay down and pulled some of the skin over himself. They were soon warm and cozy. Chingwe started to snore.

Dark Sky elbowed his grandfather in the ribs and said, "Grandfather tell us some more."

"I will tell you more tomorrow." he mumbled. "Go to sleep now."

The sound of the rain pattering against the shelter lulled them into a deep sleep. Chingwe, in his dreams, was once again a small boy playing with his friends Toti and Waupee in a carefree world, here along the banks of the Spaylawetheepi, the beautiful Ohio River.

Chingwe awoke as the sun was coming up. He prodded Dark Sky and Gray Squirrel and said. "Come boys, let's go see if we will have some fish for breakfast."

As they neared the river, Chingwe noticed that two of the saplings he had used were standing straight up with the fish lines hanging limply. The third one though was bent out over the water and the line stretched tightly into the river.

He quickly checked the first two. No fish. One had the hook missing and the other one had only the bare hook. He went to the third one and reached for the fish line. He began to pull it in and upon doing so realized he had something very large on the other end.

He pulled the line gently towards him and could feel the weight of the fish slowly beginning to give way. The fish had worn himself out struggling to escape against the whipping motion of the sapling. Dark Sky and Gray Squirrel stood bent over on the bank with their hands on their knees, peering into the water to see what their grandfather was pulling in.

Suddenly a head appeared. It was the huge head of a catfish. Startled, Squirrel almost fell into the water as the fish made one last effort to free himself. The water swirled as he whipped his tail.

Chingwe told Dark Sky to hold the line and keep the fish from moving back out into the river. Dark Sky held on for dear life as Chingwe reached down into the water and put his hands in the big fish's mouth. He pulled the fish up on the bank. The fish was nearly as large as Gray Squirrel.

Chingwe sat on the fish to keep him from squirming his way back into the water as he removed the hook from its mouth. "Go, Gray Squirrel, and fetch a big stick!"

Gray Squirrel scurried up into the woods and soon returned with a large stick. Chingwe pushed the stick through the one of the fish's gills and out its mouth. He and Dark Sky each took hold of the stick and began to drag the fish back to the campsite.

At the campsite they took a small rope and pushed it through the fish's gills and hoisted him up over a tree limb.

"Blue Feather! Fetch your skillet; we will have some fine catfish for breakfast. Boys, go and fetch some firewood and get the fire going."

Chingwe began to clean the catfish. He cut some fillets from the fish's sides and handed them to the boys who took them to Blue Feather. She placed them in the skillet and soon had them sizzling over the fire.

After they had eaten their breakfast, Dark Sky said, "Grandfather, tell us some more."

"Where did I leave off?"

"They were about to leave Fort Pitt for Philadelphia"

Chingwe sat cross legged and was filling his pipe as he began to tell his story.

"These events were told to me by my mother and father many times."

Chapter Seven

The morning sun had begun to rise over the eastern hills. The trees cast long shadows to the west and the air was heavy with moisture as the sun began to burn off the evening dew.

The wagoners hitched the reluctant oxen to the wagons. The wagons were the old Conestoga type with a canvass top and a seat big enough to hold two people.

With the exception of Bluebird only the drivers would be permitted to ride in the wagons. An advance party of three men were sent ahead to scout for potential danger and, later on in the day, hunt for game for the evening meal. From this point on they would stop only in the early evening to set up camp and prepare food. The wagons were pulled by two oxen each.

The route they were taking from Fort Pitt to Fort Bradford was called the Forbes Road. It was created through the wilderness by General Forbes to move supplies and men during his assault on Fort Duquesne.

From Fort Bradford on they would follow Indian Trails and the few roads and trails that were made by settlers. Their journey would be about three hundred miles over the Allegheny Mountain Range, through creeks and streams, across the Susquehanna River and through numerous little towns, settlements and Indian Villages.

Bumping along in the wagon, Bluebird turned to Henry and asked, “How long will it take for us to get to Philadelphia?”

Well, we made it to Fort Pitt from Philadelphia in about two weeks. Now, with the wagons laden with furs it might take three weeks or more.

It took them three days to travel Forbes Road to Fort Bedford. There they traded a few of their furs for some much needed salt. Salt was a scarce commodity at Fort Pitt and they were glad to get some here to season their meat.

They had a scare when they came upon Aliquippa's Gap, a passage way through the Appalachian hills. A party of Seneca warriors who had been cheated by an English trader were out to do mischief to any white men they encountered. Apparently they took some furs to trade with the Englishmen who gave them rum to drink before they finalized the deal. They got drunk and the trader ended up with their furs and they got nothing but hangovers from the rum they drank.

The trader had enough men to fend off the angry warriors so they decided to take out their revenge on other white men. They came upon the Cahiktodo's group and made some menacing gestures. Cahiktodo and one of the warriors from his village went out to talk to them. Cahiktodo got their assurance that they would not bother them. He had to give them a small bundle of beaver pelts to seal the agreement.

They stopped for a little while at Fort Littleton and then made their way to Fort Loudin. On the way there, one of the oxen became lame. They managed to talk the garrison commander into trading them a horse for the lame oxen. He remarked, "We could sure use the fresh meat."

Shippensburg was the first large British settlement they came to. Bluebird was amazed at all the cabins and frame houses there.

"Wait until you see Philadelphia!" said Henry. "This is nothing compared to that."

The inhabitants of Shippensburg seemed none to friendly so they moved on through the town and set up camp outside. They were visited that evening by a local minister who was intent on saving their souls before "those damn Quakers" got to them and damned them to hell.

Cahiktodo explained to the man that they were very tired and needed rest. He thanked him for his concern. "Perhaps another time we could meet with you."

The minister was adamant that he needed to preach a sermon to them this evening and save as many as possible. With a little gentle persuasion from Christopher, he finally left the camp and returned to Shippensburg.

The next leg of their journey took them through Trent's Gap and Kentin's Station. They spent the night at Kentin's Station and several of the men got drunk from rum they obtained from the English trader there.

Cahiktodo was furious and berated the men.

"How could you help defend us if we come under attack by someone intent on stealing our furs? Do you think my father would approve of this? If this happens again, you will personally feel my wrath!"

The men knew that Cahiktodo meant what he said and promised not to drink alcohol again while on this journey.

When they arrived at the settlement of York they were met by an Englishman named Hawkins who offered to buy all the furs they had and save them a trip to Philadelphia. When Cahiktodo refused his offer and explained to him that these furs belonged to the West Jersey Trading Company, he became loud and belligerent.

He tried to persuade Cahiktodo again by saying, "There are many thieves between here and Philadelphia, men who would kill you for a plug of tobacco. They can overtake you by force. Then you would have nothing! Sell them to me now and you will get a fair price."

"Look Mr. Hawkins! We are not going to sell to you. We have adequate means to defend ourselves and....."

"He was cut short by Hawkins upturned hand. "These furs will never get to Philadelphia. I know these men. They will....."

"Mr. Hawkins, are you threatening us? If you have some hidden designs to orchestrate an attack on us yourself, I warn you now. If this should occur we will pay you a visit some night and seek retribution. Now get away from our camp!"

With not so gentle persuasion this time, Christopher prodded Mr. Hawkins out of the camp and sent him on his way back to York. The guards were doubled the next few evenings.

When they arrived at Wright's Ferry on the Susquehanna River they had to load the oxen and horse onto the ferry first. Mr. Wright demanded currency for his services. Henry was prepared for that and paid him with English Shillings provided by the West Jersey Trading Company for just that purpose.

After the animals were across the river, the men had to manually load the wagons onto the ferry one at a time. It took four trips to get everyone and everything across.

Contrary to Mr. Hawkins threats, there was no attempt by anyone to ambush the party. On the evening of the twenty first day they arrived at the little settlement of White Horse. They set up camp and as they were sitting around the fire, waiting for their venison to roast Henry smiled at Bluebird.

"Bluebird, tomorrow you will get to see the great city of Philadelphia."

"Does it have as many houses and cabins as Shippensburg?" she asked.

"Not only are there more cabins and houses, there are buildings made of stone that are as high as the trees. There are streets lined with them that are over a mile long. Some of the streets are made of cobble stone."

"What about the people?"

"There many of them, more than you can count."

"Are they friendly?"

"Most are, some are not. But the people we are going to be seeing are all kind and generous. You'll see. Cahiktodo's father is one of their best traders."

"Tell me something Henry," Cahiktodo said, "All this distance we traveled, all the time we spent, all the effort that was made to get these furs and transport them here. With having to pay my father and us, how can the West Jersey Trading company make any money?"

"Cahiktodo, what they pay your father and us is just a small pittance compared to what these furs will bring on the market. There is a huge demand for them not only in the eastern cities here, but European markets across the ocean as well. The West Jersey Trading Company makes a very large profit on each fur."

Chapter Eight

Bluebird had expected to see a large town when they would eventually arrive at Philadelphia, but the sight that met her eyes as they crested the hill overlooking the city left her speechless and in awe. As she gazed down upon the city it looked to her as if it stretched from horizon to horizon. There was a pall of smoke from the many fires and chimneys hanging in the air that created a surreal vision, like something you would see in a dream.

Henry pointed towards the south east side of the city.

"Look over there Bluebird. See that row of buildings along the river? That is our destination. That row of houses and cabins that run from just below us, to those buildings is called Wharton Street. We'll be there this afternoon."

The drivers eased their wagons down the hill and entered Philadelphia. As they made their way down Wharton Street towards the Delaware River, Bluebird sat quietly in the wagon seat beside Henry. She was trying to take it all in. They passed house after house and building after building. The street was filled with people, some walking, some on horseback and others riding in wagons or carriages.

She marveled at the women dressed in fancy dresses that billowed out at the bottom making them look too large for the women. "How can they walk?" she thought to herself, "You can't tell if they have legs!"

Some of the men had hair as white as snow. "Those are powdered wigs," Henry said as he noticed her staring at a gentleman who passed by on a horse. "Can you imagine your husband wearing one of those?" She laughed.

Upon the arrival of the wagons at the warehouse, they were greeted by Joseph Miller. Joseph was the son of Adam Miller and was now the manager of the West Jersey Trading Company office in Philadelphia. He greeted them by shaking hands and welcoming them to Philadelphia.

He looked at Cahiktodo and said, "And this must be James Jr. We are so proud to meet you. Your father must be very proud of you also."

Cahiktodo returned the greeting with a hearty handshake and replied, "This is my wife Bluebird."

Joseph took Bluebirds hand and exclaimed. "Why it is a pleasure meeting you Mrs. Letart. I imagine your journey here was quite tiresome."

He was a little surprised when she answered him in perfect English. "Very tiring sir, but I enjoyed every mile of it. I saw things I never would have imagined. The country was beautiful and we had fairly decent weather. This Philadelphia is most intriguing to me. I am still in a state of awe by the many people and homes here."

Cahiktodo presented the letter of introduction, list of supplies and sundries he wanted. Mr. Miller opened the letter of introduction and began reading.

"Ah Bluebird, it says here that you are of the Lenape Nation. I have several good friends who are Lenape. My wife speaks Lenape very well. She learned it from our friends. She will be so pleased to meet you."

"You and your husband will be guests at my house while supplies for your return trip are gathered. Come, let's go there now and get something to eat."

He led them to a large buggy that was hitched to two beautiful coal black horses. Each was as black as the night sky. Bluebird walked up to one and placing her hand under his muzzle, stroked his head with the other hand. The horse snorted his approval of her action.

"These are beautiful animals Mr. Miller. I have never seen such fine horses."

The stallion you are petting is named Prince and the mare is named Princess. They are my pride and joy. They are very intelligent and are well trained."

As they entered the buggy, Joseph said, "I don't really need my driver up there but I have him so others passing by won't become alarmed. Watch this."

He leaned out the buggy door and shouted, "Home! Home my pets!"

The horses turned and started down the road towards the Miller house at a trot.

A little more than a mile after they had passed the edge of town, they came upon the Miller estate. Bluebird and Cahiktodo were taken in by the sight of this huge two story brick house with six chimneys protruding from the roof.

The horses pulled up in front of the house and a black servant came up to them and held the bridle of the stallion as the passengers stepped out of the buggy. He was the first black man that Bluebird had ever seen and she caught herself staring at him. He noticed her looking at him and held out his hand.

"Howdy ma'am, my name's De Lucious but mos' folks jes call me Luke. I'd rather they do cause De Lucious sounds like something good to eat and I don't want no one chawin' on me. I takes care of de master's horses. I hopes you had a real good trip."

Bluebird shook his hand and said "Pleased to meet you Luke."

The door of the house opened and a woman in a large billowing, yellow dress appeared and walked over to the buggy. She had graying hair and was grinning ear to ear.

"This is my wife Anne," Said Joseph. "Anne, this is James Letart's son, James Jr. and his lovely wife Bluebird."

Anne said, "I am so pleased to meet you and have you as guests at our home. I just love having company. Please come on in. Dinner is just about ready."

As they entered the house Cahiktodo's mouth began to water. The air was filled with the aroma of roast beef cooking with onions, potatoes and carrots. A black female servant met them at the door.

"This is Cassie", said Anne. "She will show you to your room and where you can clean up for dinner."

"Come on" Cassie said as she reached for the bag that Bluebird was carrying.

"I can carry this Cassie."

"No ma'am, that's my job." Cassie took the bag from Bluebird's hand, "You just follow me."

She led them up the staircase and down a long hallway to a large door. As she opened it she said, "Now, this is your room. I done cleaned it up real good for you. I even changed the sheets on the bed like the mistress told me too."

There was a fireplace on one side of the room and a huge feather bed with a canopy on the other. Bluebird walked over to the bed and asked, "Is this where we sleep?"

"What's the matter with you girl? Ain't you never seen no bed before?"

"Nothing like this!" Bluebird replied. She lay down on the bed and sank into the soft mattress. The soreness in her body from all the bumps and grinds of her traveling seemed to flow out from her.

"Oh my!" she exclaimed, "This is wonderful! I don't know if I can get back up!"

"Well you'd better get back up! Cassie exclaimed, "and go get washed up! The mistress had us fix up a big dinner for you all and if you don't go down and eat it, she'll be fit to be tied! Now they's a washroom down the hall to the right. You all go on down there and wash up then come on downstairs for dinner. I gots to get myself on down there and help in the kitchen."

As Cassie left, Cahiktodo lay down beside his wife. "We'll sleep well tonight!"

"These are such wonderful people," Bluebird said, "So warm and friendly. It is a shame that all people are not like them. The world would be such a better place."

"Come Bluebird. Let's not keep them waiting."

They got up and went to the washroom down the hall. After they washed the dust from their face and hands they walked down the stars and were met by Cassie.

"I hope you all's good and hungry! We got lots of vittles to lay out!"

She led them to the dining room. Joseph and Anne were already there and seated around a large table with their children. There were two young girls and a young lad who looked to be about fifteen or sixteen.

"These are my children", Said Joseph as he stood and motioned Cahiktodo and Bluebird to their places. This is Joseph Junior and my two daughters Elizabeth and Charity."

He pulled Bluebird's chair out from the table and in a gentlemanly manner positioned it under her as she sat down. He returned to his seat and rang a small, silver bell which was setting near his plate.

The servants entered the room carrying a large platter of roast beef, bowls filled with potatoes, onions and carrots and a large platter of fresh bread already sliced. Beside each person they sat a small bowl of butter. Next came a platter filled with sliced cucumbers, tomatoes and bell peppers.

"What would you like to drink?' Cassie asked as she carried in a large pitcher of Sassafras tea. A small black servant girl followed her carrying a pitcher of milk and a pitcher of spring water.

After the food had been set on the table and the drinks poured, Joseph said, "Anne, would you please say the blessing?"

Cahiktodo was in the process of reaching out for the platter of roast beef and looked over at Bluebird with a quizzical look on his face. Bluebird shook her head no and he withdrew his hand.

Anne and the others bowed their heads and she began.

"Dear Father in Heaven we ask that you bless this food to the nourishment of our bodies and that you bless the hands of those that prepared it. We thank you for all the many wonderful blessings you have bestowed upon us already. We thank you for allowing James and his wife a safe journey here and pray that you grant them a safe return. In the name of our Lord and Savior, Jesus Christ we pray. Amen"

"Let's eat!" James Junior exclaimed as he grabbed a slice of bread off the platter and began spreading butter on it. Soon everyone's plate was full and they were enjoying this sumptuous meal.

Anne said, "Make sure you save a little room, for Cassie has made some fresh apple pies for us today."

Cahiktodo and Bluebird had never had such a dinner as this. Everything was delicious but when Cassie brought out an apple pie, they were amazed at how good it was. They had never tasted anything like it. The cooked apples mixed with sugar, nutmeg and cinnamon were strange to their palates. They both asked for more.

The chatter around the table had originally centered on the past fight with the French. They discussed how the English control of the area would affect the fur trade.

Bluebird and Cahiktodo told of their journey up the Ohio to Fort Pitt and their overland Journey to Philadelphia. They told of their run in with Daniel Greathouse and his crew, the flock of passenger pigeons, the incidents with the Seneca and the loud mouthed sergeant at Fort Pitt.

Cahiktodo told of his meeting with Simon Girty and the warning Girty had given him of Lewis Wetzel.

Joseph said, "I have heard of this Wetzel and I consider him an outlaw and a disgrace to the British Empire. Why, I heard he even murdered a Conestoga chief who had been invited to Fort Pitt by the fort's commander. I hear he is very elusive. He needs to be captured and hanged. His actions could cause a major war with the Indians."

Anne asked Bluebird about her home. Bluebird described the peaceful little village on the Ohio River. She told of how the sound of the water going over the falls would lull her to sleep each night. She spoke of the beautiful birds and animals in the area around her village. She said that one of her favorite things about her home was all the many beautiful wild flowers that grew along the river and in the surrounding woods.

Anne said, "I too have a love for flowers. After you rest a while I'll take you to my lily garden."

Joseph said, "If you like flowers Bluebird, you will definitely enjoy Anne's lily garden. She belongs to the Botany Club in Philadelphia and her lily garden is well known throughout the county. She is a wonderful botanist. Anne has just about every kind of lily there is in her garden. She spends most of her time down there. I must say that it is one of the best kept gardens in the Philadelphia area. She has Luke and Cassie helping her. Starting in early spring and up through the summer months I rarely get to see her unless I go down there. She's always there with her lilies. They're the most important thing in her life!"

"Joseph, that's not true. I know I spend a lot of time there but you and my children hold first place in my heart."

"I'll concede to that. You do bring a lot of beauty into this world that can be so ugly at times. I am proud of you and your lilies."

"I would really like to go now!" Bluebird said excitedly, "If I should lie down to rest after this great meal, I may not be able to get up before tomorrow. I do so want to see your flowers."

Anne replied, "All right then, we'll go now.

Joseph said to Cahiktodo, "James while the ladies go to the garden, let's you and I go over the list your father sent."

Bluebird expected to see some beautiful flowers as she and Anne strolled through the woods behind the house, but she was not expecting to see the sight that befell her when they walked out into the meadow. There before her eyes was an area that covered nearly an acre, filled with lilies of every imaginable color. There were yellow ones, red ones, blue, white, purple, orange and many multi-colored ones.

Bluebird had seen wild lilies growing near her village on the river but they were nothing like the ones she now saw. Anne had laid them out in adjoining beds with a path that meandered through this field of beauty. Birds flittered through the trees and the air was filled with the buzzing of bees as they went from flower to flower collecting pollen to make their honey. It was the most beautiful place that Bluebird had ever seen.

As she and Anne walked slowly down the path, Anne would point out certain lilies and say their names. She would tell Bluebird the best times to plant the bulbs, how deep to set them and how far apart they should be. Bluebird was fascinated by her knowledge and asked many questions.

Anne asked Bluebird a question in the Lenape tongue. Bluebird answered in English and Ann said. "No, please talk to me in your language. I love the Lenape language and I would like to become fluent in it."

They spoke in Lenape for the rest of their trip through the garden. Anne spoke English only when she could not say the word or phrase in Lenape.

That day, Bluebird and Anne became good friends.

Chapter Nine

Once the ladies left the house to visit the Lily Garden, Joseph led Cahiktodo to another room and asked him to sit down. Joseph sat behind a large desk and produced the list he had received from Cahiktodo's father and uncle Jacques.

Joseph looked over the list sent by James:

3 nests copper kettles with covers
2 nests copper kettles without covers
20 iron skillets
38 rifles
12 fowling pieces
200 lbs buckshot
10 casks powder
10 boxes bar lead
10 powder horns
100 bullet molds
20 beaver traps
20 traps
100 lbs. pig tail tobacco
20 shot bags
100 fish lines with hooks
5 dozen ivory combs
20 plain tomahawks
20 pipe tomahawks
50 axes
20 pair two point blankets
20 pair three point blankets
20 calico shirts
30 yards yellow flannel
30 yards red flannel
30 yards white flannel
30 lbs vermillion

1 gross straight awls

"James," Joseph started to speak but was interrupted by Cahiktodo's raised hand.

"Please Joseph, call me Cahiktodo, I prefer my Shawnee name."

"Cahiktodo," Joseph continued, "It looks as though we have everything your father and uncle have requested. It won't take long for us to get this together and loaded on the wagons."

"Next year you won't have to travel so far. As soon as the area around Fort Pitt is settled, we plan to build a warehouse there on the point. Will you be coming back then?"

"Joseph, I must tell you this. The only reason I am here now is because my father asked me to. Both he and my uncle are in failing health. I may return, but as of now it is uncertain. I have no desire to become a trader after my father passes on. I will work at it long enough to make sure all of his accounts are settled then I will take up my life as a Shawnee."

"I am very sorry to hear that Cahiktodo. Your family has been a part of the West Jersey Trading Company since we began business here. Your grandfather James I and his wife Ann were among the first traders we employed."

"You father has many brothers and nephews continuing the trade through out the county. I was hoping you would take over your father's business and maybe even consolidating it with your Uncle Jacques' as he has no sons to pass it on to. I won't try to influence you though. I know you must follow your heart. But, perhaps one day you may change your mind."

"Regardless of your decision, you will always be welcome here, you and your lovely wife Bluebird. My wife has really taken a shine to her."

Cahiktodo said, "You and your family will always be welcome at our village if you should ever wish to travel down the river to visit us. The invitation will always be open."

"I just might take you up on that some day Cahiktodo. I've always had a desire to see the frontier. I don't know if my wife could stand the trip though. She has never been away from civilization before."

The ladies returned to the house and Bluebird ran excitedly up to Cahiktodo.

"Oh Cahiktodo, you must see this place she created. It is so beautiful! There are so many different kinds and colors of flowers!"

"All are lilies." Ann added.

Bluebird continued, "Ann said she is going to give me some bulbs to take back to the village so I can plant them. She is going to show me how to set them out and care for them tomorrow. You must come with us and see this place."

Joseph said, "You do that Cahiktodo. In the morning I will go into the warehouse and get started gathering up and loading the supplies for your return trip. I'm sure you and your wife are exhausted. Let's call it a day. I am an early riser and I firmly believe in that old saying, "Early to bed, early to rise makes a man healthy, wealthy and wise."

Cahiktodo and Bluebird went up the stairs to their room. They undressed and lay down in the feather bed. They soon were both asleep.

Cahiktodo began to dream. In his dream he was stalking a big buck deer drinking from the Ohio River above the falls near the village. As he got closer the buck saw him and quickly darted into the woods.

Cahiktodo started to give chase but pulled up as he saw a huge buck emerge from the woods with a very large rack of antlers. He was as white as snow with glowing red eyes. Cahiktodo stopped and stared at this apparition.

Soon another buck and several does stepped from the woods. All were snow white. The big buck started stamping his feet and snorting. Before Cahiktodo's eyes he transformed into a creature with the body of a deer and the head of a wolf. He bared his dripping fangs and glared at Cahiktodo.

More bucks just like him began to emerge from the woods and gather around the big one. At a bellow from the big buck, they all started running down the slope towards Cahiktodo. Snorting and shaking their lowered heads as they leapt and bound over the rocks.

Terrified, Cahiktodo started to run downriver towards the village, but there was something wrong with his legs. As hard as he tried, he could not move faster than a walk.

The herd of white deer monsters was gaining on him and he turned to fight. He loosed several arrows and managed to bring down a couple of them, but there was no stopping the big buck. As the white nightmare got closer Cahiktodo began to sing his death song. The big buck leaped into the air and with head lowered was about to gorge Cahiktodo with his huge antlers.

At that instant, Cahiktodo awoke and sat up quickly. Sweat was pouring from his brow and he was breathing heavily. He sat there for a moment, thinking about the nightmare he just awakened from. He looked over at his wife curled beside him. She was sound asleep with a smile on her face.

Bluebird was dreaming also. In her dreams she was walking in a field of lilies she had planted above the falls near the village. People from the village had come to admire her lilies and were telling her how they appreciated the beauty she had brought into their lives.

Cahiktodo lay back down and was soon asleep again. This time it was a restful sleep with no dreams.

Cahiktodo and Bluebird awoke to a gentle rapping at their bedroom door. Bluebird jumped up, draped her doeskin dress over herself and walked barefoot to the door. As she opened it she was greeted by Cassie standing there with folded arms.

"Ya'll goin' to sleep the day away? Get yourselves rousted up now and come on down and eat some breakfast. Master Joseph has done et and gone to town!"

She stuck her head in and shouted to Cahiktodo who was still lying in bed, "He said he be back around noon to fetch you Master Letart."

As she started to leave, she turned back around and said, "By the way, he said to tell you to enjoy the lilies."

"We'll be right down Cassie."

After they dressed and washed the sleep from their eyes they walked down and joined Ann and the children at the table. They enjoyed a hearty breakfast of eggs and ham fried over the fire in a large iron skillet with biscuits baked in a Dutch oven in the fireplace. They washed it down with cool milk taken from the spring house.

When they finished Bluebird asked, "Can we go to the lily garden now? I am very anxious for Cahiktodo to see it."

"Anne turned to her children and said, "While we are gone children, I want you to begin wrapping those bulbs I showed you and packing them in those crates. I will help you finish when we return. Remember, just moisten the wrapping, and don't soak them."

Cahiktodo couldn't believe his eyes when they walked out into the small meadow where the lily garden was laid out.

"They are just as beautiful as you said." He remarked to Bluebird.

"How did you come by so many different colors?" he asked Anne.

"As my husband mentioned, I am a member of the Botany Club in Philadelphia. As a matter of fact I am the president. Lilies are my love and my specialty. All of the members have donated bulbs and I obtain a lot from England and other places in the Empire. I also get some from Holland and France. I have them sent to me by ships and receive them at the harbor."

"What you see here is just a part of my collection. I have many bulbs not yet planted. I am going to give some of these to your wife. She seems to love the lilies as much as I do."

As they walked along the paths Anne told Bluebird the secrets of setting out and maintaining a lily garden.

"It is very important that you keep the bulbs moist on your journey. Do not let them dry out completely or they will not grow. Don't put too much water on them or they will die. Once you get home, you must find a place where there is no chance of flooding and where the ground is well drained. If you select the right place they will grow and multiply year after year. You will have lilies forever."

As they walked along, Cahiktodo saw a singe deer near the edge of the woods. It was a young buck and it brought to his memory the dream he had last night. The buck looked up at them and stood staring in curiosity. Cahiktodo's eyes picked up a flash of gold through the trees. It was moving quickly towards the deer.

"Panther!" he thought to himself.

The deer finally saw the approaching big cat and bolted from the edge of the woods through the lily garden with his white tail raised in alarm. He leapt and bounded effortlessly over the flower beds without disturbing a single lily.

Startled, Anne said, "Oh my, what got into that deer?"

Cahiktodo replied, "A Panther! I saw him coming down the hill. He had his eyes set on that deer. He's gone now though. He caught sight of us and ran away."

Anne said, "I've seen him before. I never come here alone and I always carry some protection."

She pulled an old flintlock pistol from the basket she was carrying and held it up for Cahiktodo to see.

"I may not hit that cat if he comes after me, but the noise this thing makes would surely scare him away."

They cut some lilies and placed them in Anne's basket. When they arrived back to the house, she put them in a large vase and sat it on the table in the dining room.

"There," she said as she stepped back to look at her work. "That brightens up the place a little."

Joseph returned a little after noon. He met Cahiktodo on the porch and told him, "The supplies have been packed and the loading of the wagons has begun. They will be ready to go this afternoon. All of your men have been informed and they are preparing to leave with you."

"That is well Joseph; we will depart in the morning."

Bluebird and Anne came onto the porch just as Cahiktodo was saying that. "Must we go so soon? Bluebird asked.

"We must make haste as my father sorely needs these supplies."

Bluebird looked disappointed. "There is much I wanted to learn from Anne about the lilies."

"Come," said Anne, "Let's you and I go back to the garden now and I will tell you more."

Anne and Bluebird spent the rest of the day at the garden, returning just before nightfall. Cassie playfully scolded them for missing supper. She jokingly said, "We done et everything and what was left we fed to the hogs! You'll have to go to bed tonight without your supper! We had a good one too, there was ham and boiled potatoes, with peas and carrots right from the garden. It's a shame too that Luke fed them hogs the last of the apple pie."

Bluebird's stomach growled loudly and Cassie and Anne began laughing.

"Don't you worry none Bluebird, I was just joking wit you. I saved you and the Missus plenty. You go on and get cleaned up and I'll set the table for you."

Laughing, she turned and scurried off to the kitchen.

"That Cassie is something else isn't she?" Anne said. "She's been with us since she was born. She's like one of the family and we love her dearly."

"Joseph bought her mother years ago when he was on a trip to Richmond. She was pregnant and died giving birth to Cassie. We raised Cassie ourselves. She is very smart, although you wouldn't know it sometimes. She reads from the Bible every night. I taught her to read and write myself. I know you're not supposed to allow the Blacks to read and write but I don't agree with that. When she was little, she had such a desire to learn and she picked it up very quickly. She even helps my children with their school work at times. No one outside the family knows about this so I must ask you to keep it to yourself."

"I would love to be able to write." Said Bluebird, "Cahiktodo taught me to speak and understand

French and English but not how to write the words. He can do it and he has told me several times that some day he will teach me."

"I noticed the tattoo on his arm." Said Anne, "LETART. I knew his Grandparents and they spelled and pronounced their surname as Letort."

"Cahiktodo's father once told me that his name in French is pronounced Letort, but for some reason people kept calling him Letart. He grew tired of correcting them and began pronouncing it Letart as well."

Anne replied, "That is interesting. I know some of his uncles and nephews who also pronounce their name Letart. The English have a way of changing the pronouncement of foreign words to suit their tongue."

Cahiktodo entered the dining room. "Come Bluebird, we must go to sleep now. We will rise with the sun. The wagons and men are ready to begin our journey home and will be waiting for us in the morning. Joseph and I took the crates of lily bulbs and loaded them on the rear of one of the wagons so you could easily get to them, just as you asked."

Anne stood up and said, "I am not an early riser like Joseph, but I too will be up to see you off in the morning. She hugged each of them. "I bid you both a good night and may you rest well."

Cassie was up well before dawn and had breakfast ready and waiting as the others came downstairs into the dining room. The children were still sleeping. After breakfast they walked outside. Luke had already hitched the horses to the buggy and was standing there waiting.

Cahiktodo turned to Anne and thanked her for her hospitality. "You and your family will always be welcome to visit Bluebird and I at our village on the Ohio."

"I would love to do that! I would like to journey down to see the garden that Bluebird is going to create."

Anne reached out to Bluebird and took her in her arms. Bluebird returned the embrace. With tears streaming down her face Anne said to Bluebird, "I will miss you Bluebird, You will always be in my thoughts and prayers. May God bless you and Cahiktodo with many children. You are a wonderful person and I know in my heart that you will create a beautiful garden at your home. When you look at your lilies, think of me and when I look at mine I will be thinking of you."

Bluebird tearfully bid Anne goodbye and begged her to come to her village some day.

"I promise to come if I am able. I am not in the best of health right now, but perhaps God will someday grant me the strength to make such a journey."

They climbed into the buggy and Joseph yelled to the horses. "To work my pets! To work!"

As the horses began to pull the buggy, Bluebird turned and waved to Anne who was standing there with her hand at her mouth. Anne stood there waving and watched as the buggy rolled out of sight.

Chapter Ten

The horses came to a stop at the entrance to the warehouse and stood quietly as the passengers climbed off the buggy. One of Joseph's workers came over and led the horses away to feed and water them.

The oxen were hitched to the wagons. Burkey and Lebeau greeted Cahiktodo and Bluebird. Burkey said, "All the men and wagons are ready to go. Just give us the command when you are ready."

Bluebird checked the crates of lily bulbs then climbed up into the seat beside Henry Weber. Joseph handed Cahiktodo a leather satchel.

"This contains letters to your father and to your uncle Jacques. Would you please see that they get them? Cahiktodo, I hope that you make the decision to follow in your father's footsteps and that you return next year."

He shook hands with Cahiktodo and continued, "I wish you a safe and uneventful journey home and may God be with you."

Cahiktodo thanked Joseph for sharing his home with them. He then turned and with a wave of his hand the driver's whipped their reins and the wagons started moving.

The journey to Fort Pitt was uneventful except for a couple of days when they were followed by a motley looking bunch of men near Shippensburg. Cahiktodo sent two of his warriors out to keep an eye on them. If their intentions were to ambush the group and steal the wagons, they must have had second thoughts once they knew they had been discovered. The scouts told Cahiktodo that they just melted into the woods. They were not seen again.

Bluebird dutifully opened the crates of bulbs every other day. They had been packed in peat moss and she made sure they stayed moist but not wet.

Upon their arrival at Fort Pitt they were met by Simon Girty. After handshakes and hellos were said all around he pulled Cahiktodo aside.

"Cahiktodo, I stayed around just to give you a warning. Trouble's brewing up and down the river and all the way up to the lakes."

"Chief Pontiac of the Ottawa and Chief Kiashuta of the Seneca are lining up tribes to fight the British. Those lyin' bastards haven't done a thing they said they were going to do after they whipped the French. They're still here and have no intention of pulling out. And what's worse, they have been treating with their allies, the Iroquois Confederation to buy land in the Ohio country. Hell, the Iroquois have no claim to any land in the Ohio country. They say they do by "right of conquest". That's a bold face lie. The British told them to say that so they can buy the land from them."

"Simon, I thought the Seneca were part of the Iroquois Confederation."

"They are, but the Ohio Seneca realized long ago what the British were all about and believe me, in the Ohio Seneca Nation there is no love for the British."

"All the Shawnee, Lenape, Mingo and Wyandots around here are ready to fight. Pontiac's got the Potawatomis, the Objibwa and Hurons pounding the war posts up along the lakes. He's even got the Miamis, Weas, Kickapoos, Mascoutons and Piankashaws from the Illinois country ready to join him."

"Beware Cahiktodo...you and your village will be affected by all this. If we don't stop them now, there will be a flood of white settlers pouring down the river and they won't stop at anything to drive you from your lands so they can settle there. Pontiac and Kiashuta aim to stop it before it starts."

"I don't know if they can pull it off, but I'm going back to my Seneca brothers and join them in their effort. Your group should not stay around here long. The British care little for Shawnee and Delaware right now and they look for any excuse to kill a red man and to get to your pretty wife, nothing short of murder will keep them from trying."

Cahiktodo took Simon's hand and said, "Thank you my friend, I know you are anxious to join your brothers. Thank you for staying to give us this warning. We will not be here for one minute longer than necessary. When this is over Simon, come to my village. You will always be welcome there."

"I will do that Cahiktodo, if I can and if the village is still there. May the spirits watch over you and your band and give you a safe journey home."

"Keep your eyes open Cahiktodo. Remember Wetzel is still around these parts somewhere. I hope that some day a brave young warrior will kill that son of a bitch and take his greasy long scalp. He's been responsible for more deaths than can be counted. Who knows, I may even try to get him myself some day. Take care Cahiktodo, I am leaving now. I hope our paths will cross again someday."

"Farewell friend."

Cahiktodo told the men to take the wagons down to the river and begin loading the canoes. They expressed a desire to stay for the night and drink some rum before they began their journey downriver. Cahiktodo forbade it.

"There will be no alcohol drunk from this point on. We must remain alert at all times. There are those who would not hesitate to attack us to steal the goods we carry."

It took the men less than two hours to unload the wagons and fill the canoes. During that time Cahiktodo told them of the warning he received from Girty. There was still a good ten hours of daylight left when they pushed off the point and floated out into the mighty Ohio River.

Cahiktodo told his men, "Today, I want to put as much distance between us and Fort Pitt as we can."

Daniel Greathouse and Bill Grills had been waiting at Fort Pitt for the wagons to arrive. When they spied their approach they immediately ran to gather up their cohorts and rushed to the river to their canoes. They pushed off and began paddling furiously downriver.

Greathouse had in mind the perfect place to spring an ambush and he wanted to get there well ahead of the flotilla's canoes laden with valuable goods.

Chapter Eleven

Burkey's canoe led the flotilla down the Ohio River with Lebeau's canoe guarding the rear. About thirty miles downriver, near the mouth of Yellow Creek, was a village of Mingo Indians. Their Chieftain was named Logan. He took this name in honor of James Logan, a friend of his father Shikellamy.

Logan, like his father, was always a peace advocate and a friend of the white, French or English as well as all Indian Nations. He and his village took no part in the confrontation between the English and the French in the past war. He had lived for a while in Philadelphia as a child and it was there that he and Christopher Burkey became childhood friends.

Burkey beached his canoe at the mouth of Yellow Creek and waved the others to do the same. Logan and several members of his family came down to the beach to welcome the travelers. Recognizing Burkey he shook his hand and embraced him.

"It is good to see you my old friend, you are looking well. You are all welcome here."

Burkey introduced Cahiktodo and Bluebird. Logan shook their hands as well as the hands of every member of the party.

"Come, all of you. We will eat and talk. I will send some of my men to guard your canoes."

Cahiktodo looked at Burkey and started to object but Burkey took him by the arm and said, "We can trust him and his people, the goods will be safe, I assure you."

Logan led the group up over the bank to his village where they were welcomed by the villagers who crowded around them.

“You came at the right time.” Said Logan, “We are about to have a feast in honor of several young boys who have just become men.”

The women were roasting venison over open fires and had vegetables cooking in large iron pots suspended from poles.

Logan asked Burkey how he had fared over the years and Burkey told him how he had been hired by the Letart family in their trading business.

“I know the Letart name,” Said Logan. “They have a reputation of fairness and honesty in their dealings with all the nations.”

He looked at Cahiktodo and asked, “What is that strange marking on your arm?”

Cahiktodo held his arm up and said, “This is my French name, Letart. My father had it tattooed on my arm when I was just a child. He told me he wanted me never to forget my French heritage.”

“Is your father Jacques Letart?

“No, Jacques is my uncle. My father is James. I have some supplies for my uncle on the canoes. He has a trading post upriver from my father’s.”

“I know Jacques very well. He and my father were good friends. He spent a lot of time at our cabin near Philadelphia. I would like to see him again.”

Burkey asked, “Why don’t you journey downriver with us and visit?”

“Yes, Said Bluebird, “You and your wife could stay at our village on the falls.”

“I will consider that,” replied Logan. “My wife will not be able to go for my oldest daughter is about to bear us a grandchild. My wife will want to be here when that happens. I will give you my answer in the morning.”

Everyone ate their fill and one by one they retired. Burkey and Logan talked late into the night, reminiscing about their childhood.

The next morning Logan told Bluebird and Cahiktodo, "I will accept your invitation and accompany you down to visit Jacques."

Cahiktodo presented Logan with a rifle and a powder horn from his supplies. "These are gifts to you on behalf of my father and me for your hospitality."

Logan took the rifle and looked it over. He thanked Cahiktodo. "This is a fine rifle. I will take it with me on our journey."

Accompanied by two warriors from his village, Logan packed some supplies into a canoe and once they were all aboard, the flotilla pushed off. Logan's canoe traveled beside Burkey's war canoe and the two continued their reminiscing as the proceeded down the gently flowing river.

After a few days had past with no sign of trouble, Lebeau sped his war canoe forward. As he passed Burkey he said, "We are going on ahead to find a campsite and do a little hunting. "

"Be careful," Said Burkey, "And stay alert!"

"You can count on that," replied Lebeau, "I have a feeling we will run into those ruffians we met coming upriver again. We'll meet up with you downriver a ways."

Lebeau and his men paddled briskly and were soon well ahead of the flotilla. Lebeau saw a spot that looked suitable for a campsite and they steered the canoe into shore. Once they beached the canoe, two of the men went into the woods to hunt. Lebeau and the other man went ashore and began to scout out the campsite and gather wood for fires.

The rest of the flotilla came upon the site a while later and they beached their canoes beside Lebeau's. They began building quick shelters and fires and soon the two hunters appeared out of the woods. Each hunter carried two turkeys and between them on a large pole was tied the carcass of a large buck.

The sat the deer down and one of them dropped his turkeys and walked up to Cahiktodo.

"We round something back there," he said, "we came upon an abandoned campsite. The fire pits were not very old. There were signs of many men."

He reached into his shirt and pulled out a broken powder horn with the initials RGB carved on it. "We found this."

Burkey and Logan walked up and examined the powder horn. "This is a bad sign." Burkey said. "We had better warn everyone to be alert and double the guards."

Cahiktodo said, "We will stay here all day tomorrow. I will send some men ahead to scout out the river in front of us."

The two hunters and the two warriors from Logan's village, Genesee and Kaske, volunteered to do this.

Early the next morning the scouts climbed into Logan's canoe and pushed off. They let the current carry them, paddling only to maintain their course. They didn't want to make any noise that might alert anyone ahead they were coming.

About a mile from the camp, they beached the canoe and Logan's two warriors, Genesee and Kaske stealthily entered the woods along the shoreline. They separated and Kaske began to search the ground for signs while keeping the river in sight. Genesee moved deeper into the woods and began to search there. They quietly and slowly made their way downriver.

The men in the canoe re-entered the current and drifted along searching the bank for sign.

Back in camp, the men spent their time hunting and preparing themselves for what they considered an inevitable run in with the river pirates. They melted some of the lead bars and made extra balls for their rifles. Cahiktodo and Logan made sure everyone had a full horn of powder and extra flints.

Bluebird was moistening her lily bulbs when Cahiktodo approached. She looked up at him and said, "I am frightened Cahiktodo. What are we going to do?"

Cahiktodo sat down beside her and said, "We know not what tomorrow will bring, but we will be prepared for whatever happens. Who knows, we may not even run into these men. It is alright to be afraid Bluebird, but turn that fright into preparedness. Look for the best and expect the worst. I have confidence in myself and the men with us that we will be able to handle any situation that may arise. We will protect you Bluebird. With my life I will protect you from harm in any way."

As the sun came up the next morning, Cahiktodo, Logan, Burkey and Lebeau were discussing whether to head on downriver or wait for the scouts to return. They decided to wait until noon. Then, if the scouts had not returned they would proceed downriver with caution.

Around ten o'clock one of the men guarding the canoes ran into camp and yelled, "They are coming, the scouts are coming!"

Cahiktodo hurriedly made his way to the river and was soon joined by the others. They watched the canoe making its way upriver towards them. "I see only three men," Logan said.

Lebeau replied, "It's one of your warriors that's missing."

As the scouts beached their canoe and climbed out, one of them said, "We found em! We counted 22 men, all white."

"Genesee came upon them and managed to get close enough to their camp to hear some of them talking. They're planning to set up an ambush at the three islands above the Muskingum. From what he heard they figure we will stay in the current that runs between the first island and the Ohio shore. They plan to put some men in the woods and some on the island to catch us in crossfire as we pass."

"Genesee stayed behind to watch them and let us know if their plans change. He is going to meet us by a big rock along the river about a mile above the islands. He told us to tell you not to pass that point until he meets us there."

The men climbed into their canoes and with Burkey and Lebeau's canoes leading the way, they paddled downriver. As they rounded a small bend in the river they came upon the large rock where Genesee told them to wait. They beached their canoes and waited quietly for his appearance.

After an hour or so, Genesee came out of the woods and motioned Cahiktodo and Logan to approach him. As they reached him, he squatted down and with a stick drew a picture of the three islands in the sand.

"Just below the islands," he said, "is a small creek. They have positioned three canoes there and as far as I can tell plan to man them with three men each. The rest will spread out on this island and along the shore here. They are going to wait until we reach a certain point then open fire."

"The canoes in the creek will enter the river and block our escape. They plan on killing all of us and capturing the supplies. They are expecting us tomorrow."

"You have done well." Said Cahiktodo, "Logan, you must be proud of this warrior."

"That I am!" replied Logan as he put his hand on Genesee's shoulder, "We will talk of his bravery around the fires for a long time."

Cahiktodo had all the men pull the canoes well up onto the shore and gathered them around him. He related to them the information he received from Genesee.

"We have two choices." He said, "We could sneak by them under cover of night, past the farthest island out or, we could turn their ambush on them and attack.

"If we take the first choice we will probably have to deal with them again further down the river. They seem very determined to attack us and steal these goods."

"If we choose to attack them, we may be able to force them to give up their idea of attacking and harassing us all the way home. What do you say men, which choice should we make?"

"I think we should attack and give those bastards a taste of what they were going to give us!" Burkey exclaimed, "We don't want to have to deal with the likes of them all the way home!"

All of the men agreed.

"We will make a plan of attack then." Cahiktodo said.

He, Logan, Burkey and Lebeau walked up the shoreline to discuss their options.

"We have more men than they do," said Logan. "I propose that, under cover of darkness, we send half of our men inland to come up from behind and attack the ambushers on the shore. The other half, we'll land on the far side of the island and attack the ambushers from behind there."

"What about the canoes in the creek? Cahiktodo asked.

"I will take Kaske and one of your warriors with me. We will float downriver from the creek. Once passed the creek, we will go ashore and make our way back upriver to fire on them. My shot will be the signal for everyone to attack."

"This will keep the pirates in the canoes occupied and perhaps cause those ambushers on the island and shore to give away their positions. They will hear our fire and attempt to see what is happening to their friends in the canoes."

"We will not fire until ample time has passed for our men to get themselves into position for the attack."

"That is a good plan." Cahiktodo said, "Let's go and tell the men what we are going to do and what we expect of them."

The men spent the rest of the day eating and napping. No fires were built as the smoke might alert the ambushers to their presence. They removed supplies from some of the canoes to so they could use them to transport themselves to the island.

Cahiktodo went to Bluebird and handed her a small flintlock pistol and showed her how to load and operate it. "You will stay here. This pistol is for you just in case things don't go as planned."

"If an hour passes after the firing stops and we do not return, you must take one of the canoes and go upriver to Logan's village. Do not come downriver for any reason."

Tearfully she protested, "I can't leave you Cahiktodo, if you should be killed, I want to die too!"

"Bluebird, I have no intention of dying. I just want to be sure that you will be safe and I'll know where to find you if this fails. I don't believe we will fail, but I want you to be prepared just in case."

He kissed her lightly on her forehead and she put her arm around his neck and pulled him to her. They embraced and she said, “You must be careful, my love. I have something to tell you. I was going to wait until we reached the village to be sure, but I am now almost certain I am again with your child. I am well passed my time and my heart tells me there is another life inside me. You must return to me!”

A feeling of inexplicable joy filled Cahiktodo’s breast. “Is it a boy or a girl?” he blurted out.

Bluebird laughed and said, “We won’t know that until the child is born, only the spirits know for sure.”

“Now I have more reason to make you understand not to come down the river. I will be very cautious and alert in this fight. Nothing will stop me from seeing my child. Little Chingwe will be excited when he finds out he is going to have a little brother or sister. I would not miss that for anything.”

As the sun set and darkness overtook the earth, those that were selected to attack the island ambushers along with Logan with his warriors, manned their canoes and pushed out into the river. It was around midnight.

There was no breeze and the evening air was cool. This caused a light fog to rise on the river and hang a few feet above the water line, masking their movement as they glided silently along the far side of the river. They carefully and gently dipped their paddles to push their canoes through the water as quietly as possible letting the current do most of the work.

The rest of the men were led inland by Genesee. After a while he turned them downriver and they made their way through the dark woods to set up their positions behind the ambushers on the Ohio shore.

Logan had told the men in the canoes to beach them as quickly and quietly as possible. Once the canoes were hidden from sight, they were to spread out and move silently through the woods to about halfway across the island towards the ambushers and wait for his signal.

Once the canoes were beached and the men began moving into position, Logan and the two warriors accompanying him made their way past the third island and quietly picked up the current.

They drifted past the creek and let the current carry them about a half mile before they turned their canoes to the Ohio shore. Upon beaching the canoe and hiding it in the underbrush, they began working their way quietly back upriver towards the creek.

Logan and his two warriors crept up to the edge of the creek and saw three canoes. They were beached on the other side and there was no one around. Logan motioned for his men to lay quietly in the brush. They watched and waited.

The decision had been made last night to wait until the morning sun was well up in the sky before they began their attack. This would give all the attackers ample time to get into position. Logan's shot would be the signal to attack.

As the sun came up, Greathouse, Grills and four other men came to the creek and climbed into the canoes. They pushed off and Greathouse motioned the other two canoes to stop. He paddled his canoe out to the mouth of the creek and a little ways into the river. They were looking upstream.

They soon returned to the other canoes and Greathouse said, "They ain't comin' yet."

Grills said, "This is gonna be good, It'll be like shooting fish in a barrel"

Greathouse said, "Only if those dumb sons-of-bitches don't open fire too soon! I tell you right now, if one of them does that, I'll skin his ass and feed him to the fishes! We should have picked better men for this!"

"What if they don't come this way? Grills remarked. "What if they go between the other islands?"

"Judas Priest Grills! You're about as dumb as the rest of these bastards. What in the hell would they go that way for? The current goes here! They're packin' a lot of stuff and they're gonna take the easiest way! Now let's put Baker here out on that point so he can keep watch for em."

They paddled the canoe over to the shore and told Baker to get out and wait at the mouth of the creek.

"You tell us as soon as you see 'em comin or I'll put a ball between your eyes you sorry lookin' son-of-a-bitch! And don't you go fallin' asleep up there or I'll take your scalp! Ya hear?"

Baker climbed up to the top of the bank and made his way to the mouth of the creek. He sat down and leaned his back up against.

"I meant what I said Baker, don't you be takin' a nap up there!"

About fifteen minutes passed when Grills yelled up at Baker. "Seen anythin' yet?"

Baker stood up and turned to answer when his eye caught the glint of the sun reflecting off something on the other bank. He stood, shaded his eyes and stared across the creek, trying to make out what caught his eye.

Logan knew they had been discovered and fired his rifle. The ball caught Baker in the chest and sent him sailing backwards into the river. The other two warriors fired and one of the balls creased Greathouse's neck, causing him to yell and the blood to run down his shirt.

Firing and screaming broke out upriver along both shorelines as the attackers swooped down on the ambushers.

The men in the canoes all returned fire towards Logan and his warriors without hitting any of them. As soon as they fired, they dropped their rifles in the bottom of the canoes and began paddling frantically to the shore.

They scrambled up the bank as Logan and his warriors reloaded and fired another round. Three frontiersmen were killed in that volley but Greathouse, Grills and the others made it to the top of the bank and disappeared into the woods.

Several of the ambushers along the island and Ohio shore were killed or wounded when the attackers first opened fire. Some of the ambushers spun around and returned fire but most of them just threw their rifles down and jumped in the river to escape the screaming attackers pouring down the hillsides towards their position.

Back at the creek, only Greathouse and Grills stayed long enough to return fire at Logan. Logan and the two warriors stood to fire one more volley before they went down river to fetch their canoe. As soon as they fired, Greathouse, cursing and yelling, stepped out into the clearing and fired a shot in Logan's direction. Logan felt the air and heard the whistling sound as the ball passed by his ear and struck a tree behind him.

Greathouse stood there, shaking his fist at Logan and challenged him to fight one on one. "You red skinned son of a bitch, Com'on and fight me like a man! You bush-whackin' bastard!"

Logan shouted back, "I'll let you live this time, but I warn you. If you trouble these people again, I will hang your scalp outside my cabin door."

"Come get it now, you worthless piece of cow dung, I'm ready for you, Com'on!"

Logan smiled at Greathouse and turned to follow his warriors to the canoe.

This infuriated Greathouse. As Grills walked up to him he said, "Com'on Grills, let's go round up what sorry sons-of-bitches we got left. I know that redskin...I know where he lives. I'll have my revenge. He ain't getting away with this! I'll make him pay or my name ain't Daniel Greathouse!"

After the firing stopped, Bluebird waited as she was told, her heart in her throat. She had climbed into a canoe and pushed it out into the river. She paddled against the current to keep it from carrying her downstream. She sighed in relief and began crying as a canoe came into sight. In the bow was Cahiktodo, waving at her.

The group had suffered no casualties in the fight. They let the ambushers who panicked and jumped in the river escape. They had no desire to kill them. Cahiktodo figured they learned their lesson and would not bother them again. They didn't even pick up the rifles the ambushers threw down as they fled. They left them where they lay thinking those men would need them to hunt. Such was the mercy these men showed.

After the fight with these river pirates, Logan had second thoughts about journeying on with the flotilla. He expressed concerns for the safety of his family after this encounter. He announced that he would delay his visit and return to his village. He promised to make the trip down river sometime the next spring if he was able.

"Grandfather", Blue Feather asked, "Did Bluebird have the baby?"

"No," replied Chingwe, "it was a false pregnancy. I was the only child they ever had."

"Grandfather," Asked Dark Sky, "Did Chief Logan visit the village that next spring?"

"No, he did not as war broke out between the nations and the British. Logan and his village remained neutral in that fight, still trying to set up talks between the combatants and still welcoming anyone visiting or passing by their village with open arms. He stayed near his people during those times, constantly working for peace. My father and most of the warriors in our village remained neutral also."

Chingwe continued his story.

It was not until about ten years later that he made his visit. I remember the occasion well. My father said he was not the same man he met before. He had moved his village to the mouth of Yellow Creek and while away Daniel Greathouse kept his promise of revenge.

Greathouse and his cohorts went to Yellow Creek and killed all of Logan's family, His mother, daughter, brother, sister and his grandchild. Logan's youngest daughter Toonay was about to give birth to another child when she was killed. She was tortured and the baby cut from her body. Greathouse and his men killed and scalped over twenty Mingo men, women and children including the unborn child which Greathouse, with his tomahawk, hacked from the body of Toonay.

This changed Logan from a merciful and peace loving person into a revenge seeking warrior. He and a war party of Mingo and Shawnee warriors attacked white settlements and killed many, including women and children. He asked my father to join him but my father declined because my grandfather was near death and he wanted to be there when it happened. Logan told my father he understood.

I was a mere boy, but I wanted to go and help Logan. I felt much sorrow for him. My father would not allow it saying I wasn't old enough or experienced enough to be a help and I would just be in the way

Christopher Burkey, the Englishman and childhood friend of Logan was beside himself with outrage over what Greathouse and his men had done to his friend.

"We should have killed them all that day on the river!"

He bade my father and my grandfather farewell and joined Logan's war party. He was never seen again.

"That makes me sad also." Blue Feather said, "The white people are so cruel and evil."

Not all white people are like that Blue Feather. Some are good and kind. There are bad people in all races. Some of our own Shawnee and Lenape warriors were notorious for their cruelty. You can't judge a whole race by the actions of a few. My father and mother taught me this.

The Governor of Virginia sent men named Croghan and McKee to talk to the Indians of the Ohio country and offer his condolences as to what happened to Logan's family and try to talk them into not seeking revenge against the settlers in Virginia. Cornstalk, Chief of the Shawnee was offended by this and the fact that the Governor did not come himself, He sent a letter to these men.

Brothers,

We have received your Speeches by White Eyes, and as to what Mr. Croghan and Mr. McKee says, we look upon it all to be lies, and perhaps what you say may be lies also, but as it is the first time you have spoke to us we listen to you, and expect that what we may hear from you will be more confined to truth than what we usually hear from the white people. It is you who are frequently passing up and down the Ohio, and making settlements upon it, and as you have informed as that your wise people have met together to consult upon this matter, we desire you to be strong and consider it well. Brethren: We see you speak to us at the head of your warriors, who you have collected together at sundry places upon this river, where we understand they are building forts, and as you have requested us to listen to you, we will do it, but in the same manner that you appear to speak to us. Our people at the Lower Towns have no Chiefs among them, but are all warriors, and are also preparing themselves to be in readiness, that they may be better able to hear what you have to say. You tell us not to take any notice of what your people have done to us; we desire you likewise not to take any notice of what our young men may now be doing, and as no doubt you can command your warriors when you desire them to listen to you, we have reason to expect that ours will take the same advice when we require it, that is, when we have heard from the Governor of Virginia.

"We must go and find something to eat tonight. Boys, why don't you go down to the river and set out the fish lines again. I will go into the woods and see if I can get us a turkey."

"Blue Feather, you stay here and keep an eye on the camp. We'll be back soon and I will tell you more this evening."

Chapter Twelve

The boys managed to catch six nice catfish by fishing with the lines held in their hands from the bank. Chingwe returned without a turkey but searching around a pile of fallen rocks he found the den of a very large opossum. He clubbed the animal to death and brought it back to the campsite. He congratulated the boys on their catch and said. "Tonight we will have catfish for our supper and possum for breakfast. We will roast the possum in the coals over night."

"Grandfather," Blue Feather said, "tell us about your childhood here and what it was like."

When my father and mother returned from their trip to Philadelphia, Bluebird was anxious to plant the lilies they brought with them. She used the knowledge she learned from her friend Anne to find a place suitable to plant them.

Just above the falls was a flat topped area that never flooded when the spring rains made the river rise. It was there she decided to create her field of lilies.

I and my friends, Toti and White Hawk, helped her plant those bulbs. We cleared out brush and trees for her. She wanted to have pathways winding through the field like her friend Anne had so we gathered stones to lay them out. We worked very hard. We cleared an area so large that none of us boys could throw a rock from one end to the other.

Once we got everything cleared and the brush burned my mother showed us how to work the soil and set out the bulbs. It took us days and days to get them all into the ground. As the autumn leaves began to fall, we finally finished.

Toti and White Hawk were good friends, I will always remember them and the good times we had as children. We would hunt, fish, and play games together.

One of my favorite games was "Snowsnake". We played this game in the winter after a heavy snow. We would make a long trench in the snow and pour water in it. After the water froze we would take turns hurling a long spear down the trench. Whoever made it slide the farthest would win.

In the springtime, all the young boys and girls in the village would play a game called Pahsaheman. When we played this game, most of the village would turn out to watch. Sometimes the older men and women would play.

In this game there was a large field with goal lines on either end. There would be a ball made from deerskin filled with deer hair. The girls would be allowed to pick up the ball and run with it or throw it to another girl as the boys tried to knock it from their hands or prevent it from being thrown across the goal line.

The boys were not allowed to throw the ball or run with it. The only way they could move the ball towards their goal line was to kick it. They could kick it towards another boy and he would be allowed to catch it, but he could not run with it. He would have to drop the ball to kick it to another boy or across the goal line.

The girls were permitted to grab the boys and even knock them to the ground to get the ball, but the boys were not allowed to do that to a girl.

Someone, usually an older woman from the village, would keep score using a pile of twelve sticks. Whenever a goal was made, they would remove a stick from the pile and place it in a spot designated for each team. When the last stick was removed they would total the sticks for each team. Whoever had the most sticks won the game. In case of a tie, the first team to score a goal won.

My friend Toti was a prankster. He would play jokes on anyone, which got him in trouble a few times.

One day Toti said to me and White Hawk, “Before the New Fire Dance there is going to be a game of Pahsaheman. I have a plan. You will see something very funny happen during the game.”

“What are you going to do?” I asked.

“You will see.”

That night Toti crept into the wigwam of the old woman who kept the Pahsaheman ball and stole it. He used that ball to make one that looked just like it, only instead of stuffing it with deer hair he put in a large rock and some straw. He sewed up his ball and did such a good job that you could not tell one from the other unless you lifted them.

In our village was a Shawnee boy named Mikwa, the Bear, who was very mean. He would pick on younger children and one day, as Toti was going into the woods to relieve himself, Mikwa sprung from the underbrush and tackled him.

Mikwa wrestled him to the ground and wrapped his legs around Toti’s middle and locking his ankles together he began to squeeze.

“Come on little frog, I want to see if a frog can cry!” Mikwa increased the pressure but Toti didn’t cry, but he did wet his breach cloth.

Mikwa began laughing. “I didn’t know frogs could pee like that!”

Struggling to free himself from his attacker’s grip Toti saw his chance. He raised his arm and brought it down with as much force as he could muster. He drove his elbow into Mikwa’s groin. Mikwa released his legs from around Toti and curled up on the ground moaning.

Toti reached down and picked up a large stick and was about to strike Mikwa with it, when Mikwa jumped up and grabbed Toti. He picked Toti up and threw him into the creek.

"Go there, you filthy little frog! You need to take a bath! You stink!"

Laughing, Mikwa turned and walked back toward the village. Toti vowed that someday he would take vengeance on Mikwa.

After Toti made his look-alike ball, he snuck back into the old woman's wigwam and returned the original.

On the day of the game, Toti wore a large doeskin shirt much too big for him, but he wore it so he could hide the ball he made under his armpit. He looked funny as his left arm seemed to stick out from his body. No one seemed to notice though and only White Hawk and I knew what he was planning to do.

There were to be two games that day. The first was between the boys and a team of girls and old women of the village. The second was to be between the men and the younger women of the village.

The old grandmother brought the ball out to the center of the field and called for the boys and girls to gather around.

When both teams were present she threw the ball straight up into the air as high as she could. One of the village girls managed to catch the ball and started running towards her goal.

White Hawk was standing between her and her goal and managed to knock the ball from her hand. There was a mad scramble as everyone tried to get to the ball.

Toti dived and landed on top of the rolling ball and was immediately buried by several girls who tried to pull him up from the ground. They were pulling his hair and limbs trying to move him off the ball.

As this was going on, Toti somehow managed to switch the balls. He rolled over and saw Mikwa running towards him. He stood and rolled the ball on the ground towards the approaching Mikwa.

Mikwa kicked the ball while in a full run. Instead of the ball sailing towards the boy's goal as Mikwa expected, it only went a few feet.

Mikwa yelled and tumbled to the ground. He sat up, with tears streaming down his face and clutched his foot. He took off his moccasin and two of his toes were dangling down. Screaming and crying he rocked back and forth on his butt while holding his foot with both hands.

Toti ran over to him and said, "Mikwa, I didn't know bears could cry like that!"

Mikwa lunged and grabbed for Toti's legs, but Toti avoided him easily. A lot of the children, both boys and girls ran up to Toti and patted him on his back for his deed. Almost all of them at one time or another had been the victim of Mikwa.

Toti loved to laugh and would go to great extremes sometimes to pull a prank on someone. He pulled one on me once that still brings a chuckle to this day.

Toti, White Hawk and I planned to go on a hunting and fishing trip. We would spend several days and nights. We set up our camp at Sikona Yapewi, the big rock I showed you when we first came here.

Toti, with the help of White Hawk had taken a bearskin that belonged to Toti's grandfather and stuffed it with grass and straw, sewing it with rawhide.

They begged, borrowed and stole some lengths of rope and fish line from people in the village. They carried that stuffed bearskin to Sikona Yapewi and hid it in the brush up on the hill.

They tied the lengths of rope together and coiled it up beside the "bear". The last 20 feet or so was made up of the fish line tied together.

On the first evening of our trip, we set up a camp on the river's edge by the big rock. We built a fire and as darkness fell, we sat around it and talked.

Toti said, "My uncle, who lives over at Old Town, told me that a few days ago some boys of that village were camping near a creek when a huge black bear came out of the woods and attacked them. The bear killed all three boys and ate one of them."

"I heard that." said White Hawk, "And my father said that not too long after that, the bear attacked a small girl near the village and ate her as well."

Toti continued, "My uncle said that some of the men from the village went out to hunt down the bear and kill it, but they were not able to get close enough. They spotted the bear and tracked it for a while. He said it was last seen heading towards our village."

We were armed with just bows and arrows, not much good against a raging bear and the thought of one charging down the hill behind us sent a chill up my spine.

"Maybe we should go back to the village," I said.

"What's the matter Chingwe, are you scared?"

"No, but what can we do if that bear should come here?"

"We'll jump in the river and swim up to the village," said White Hawk.

"But what if he doesn't give us time? What if he sneaks up on us and attacks before we have a chance to escape?"

"He can't kill all of us at once! Two will be able to get away." Toti said.

"And who will those two be?" I asked.

"The two fastest." replied White Hawk.

"Let's talk about something else," said Toti, "That bear is probably nowhere near here. He's probably still near Old Town where he got some easy meals. I am sorry I brought this up. I didn't mean to scare everyone and ruin our trip."

We talked well into the night. We told stories and jokes and laughed a lot, but in the back of my mind, I kept imagining that big old bear breaking through the woods behind us and attacking. We turned in around midnight but I didn't sleep very well, I kept hearing noises up in the woods. I was glad when the sun broke over the hills and the darkness melted away.

We spent the next day, swimming and hunting. I managed to bring down a small doe with my bow and that evening we enjoyed roasted venison over our fire.

I had spent a lot of time gathering firewood that day. I wanted to have a big fire for the night.

After we had eaten and the sun went down again, darkness enveloped us and the thoughts of that bear came back to my mind. I didn't talk about it though, I would remain on alert and be prepared if an attack did come.

Toti reached into the fire and took out a burning stick to use as a torch. "I am going to go relieve myself." He said as he walked back towards the woods in the darkness.

I watched him carrying his torch and disappear into the woods behind us. I was thankful for the glow of light from the fire.

While Toti was in the woods, he grabbed the coil of rope and began to come back to our fire. He stopped and tied the fish line around his ankle so it would not be visible to me as he approached.

He sat down next to the fire and as we talked, he carefully untied the fish line from his ankle. An hour passed as we talked and at a signal from Toti, White Hawk distracted me with conversation. Toti reached out and picked up a rock. He threw the rock backwards over his head up into the woods. The sound of the rock striking the ground and rolling down the hill caught my attention.

"What was that?" I shouted as I stood up and stared into the darkness towards the woods behind us."

"What was what? White Hawk asked, "I didn't hear anything."

"Nor did I", said Toti.

"I heard something in the woods up there!" I can't believe you didn't hear it! It could be that bear stalking us!"

"Oh Chingwe, Toti said, "There's nothing up there. I was just up there a short while ago, I saw nothing! Sit down and tell us about your father's trip to Philadelphia."

I turned and sat back down. I nervously began telling of my father's journey. When I wasn't looking, Toti let fly with another rock

"There!" I shouted as I jumped up and grabbed my bow. Did you hear it that time?"

"Chingwe, what is the matter with you? Toti asked. "I heard nothing up there. Did you White Hawk?"

"Nothing, not a thing."

"Chingwe, you are letting your fear of that bear get the best of you. You are hearing things. You are just frightened....."

"I am not a coward!" I yelled, "There is something up there."

"It is just your fear!" said White Hawk.

"It is not my fear, I am not afraid. I just don't want to be taken unawares."

"Then take your bow and go up there and check it out so we can have some peace."

“Who will go with me?” I asked.

“Go yourself,” said Toti, “You are the one who is so afraid he is hearing things. I know there is nothing up there.”

“I am not afraid” I yelled angrily. “Stop saying that!”

“If you are not afraid, then go on and check out the area.”

“As I started up the hill into the darkness, Toti said. “Here, take this torch to light your way.”

“He handed me the torch and I started walking slowly into the woods. My heart was pounding. I fully expected to see a bear spring from somewhere in front of me.

The flickering light being cast from the torch reflected off the trees and brush in front of me making everything look like it was moving.”

“I looked back at the campsite. White Hawk and Toti were standing together by the fire looking at me.

“Yell if you see anything!” Toti shouted.

I walked a little way into the woods. Toti and White Hawk took hold of the fish line and began pulling on it until it was tight.

“Be careful!” they shouted as I went up the hill, deeper into the darkness. “Watch out for that bear!”

“Now!” said Toti to White Hawk.

They began to rapidly pull the line towards them. The “bear” that was attached to the other end of the line, came bolting out of the underbrush where they had hidden it and right towards me. In the glow of my torch all I could see was a blur of black fur and the noise it made being pulled through the leaves and brush sounded like it was running.

I screamed and threw down my torch and bow. I turned and ran as fast as I could back down the hill towards the campsite. Stumbling and falling over the rocks as I raced down the hill I could imagine that bear gaining on me. I could hear him behind me. I felt his breath on the back of my neck. I was expecting any second to feel his weight on my back and his fangs sinking into my flesh.

"Quick!" shouted Toti, "Into the river!"

I was not paying any attention to those two as I tripped and stumbled down the hill. Running as fast as my legs could carry me, I was intent on reaching the safety of the river. I knew that bear was right on my heels. I ran out onto the flat rock and dove out as far as I could.

Still full of fear as the cold water of the river enveloped me, I kicked as hard as I could to get back to the surface. In my mind I could see the bear on top of one of my friends, biting and tearing at him. As I kicked my way to the surface I thought I would hear the screams and growls of the attack. When my head broke the surface, Instead, I heard laughter.

There, standing on the rock, holding the stuffed bearskin was Toti. He shouted, "Here is your bear Chingwe. We killed it for you, come on out of the water now and let's eat it."

White Hawk was laughing so hard that he fell down and was rolling on the flat rock. At first I was filled with anger. Then when I realized all the effort that went into this and how comical I must have looked to them, I began to laugh too. It was a good prank, one that we spoke of for years.

My friends and I would sometimes go into the woods and wait for someone to come along. We would playfully ambush them. It did not matter if they were children or adults. When we would ambush an older male they would usually just smile and tell us what we did wrong or what we did right. We became very good at this.

One spring morning my mother woke me up and told me to go get my friends and meet her at the lily field. When we arrived she showed us how to loosen the soil around the bulbs and plants to help them grow.

"Once they get started," she said, "they will grow on their own and make more flowers."

We didn't mind helping her work in the lily field for as we worked she would tell us stories. She told stories of her father, my father and my grandfather, stories of her life experiences and many, many more. We were fascinated with her re-telling of the old days.

She would also teach us songs and we would sing them while we worked. She had a beautiful voice. She taught us to speak and understand the English language and a little French. I learned a lot from my mother, there in that field of lilies.

As spring moved on, those lilies sprang from the ground and by late spring the whole area was green with their leaves and stalks

By the middle of summer the whole field was ablaze with so many different colors and the air was filled with the sweet scent of their blossoms.

The people from the village would come to the field to see this sight and they praised my mother and us for creating such a beautiful place.

It wasn't long before word of this place got around and people would journey here from other villages just to see this wonder. Some came from as far away as the villages up on the Scioto.

My father and grandfather were so proud of my mother and her lily field. When my grandfather and grandmother passed away, they buried them up there in that lily field. They planted bulbs all over their graves.

Chapter Thirteen

"Pontiac and Kiashuta efforts to drive the British out had failed but they did get some concessions from the British government. Although the British maintained forts west of the Appalachians no white people were to be allowed to settle in the Ohio Country or so they said.

For a while there was an aura of peace in the air but the warning that my father received from Simon Girty soon proved to be true.

My grandfather's trading post was located on the Virginia side of the river. He and my grandmother had both died just after Logan's visit and the trading post was now in the hands of Jean Lebeau. My father had no desire to follow in the footsteps of his father and become a trader so he gave everything to Lebeau.

White settlers began to build their cabins and clear away land for farming on that side of the river. One settler even built his cabin on the Ohio just north of the mouth of the Kanawha. The area up the Kanawha, clear into the heart of the Appalachians soon held many cabins and farms of the white settlers.

Whites were even moving into the Cantukee lands which were held sacred by all the tribes in the area as well as the Cherokee to the south. The Cantukee lands were like a middle ground to the Indians. No tribe was permitted to take up residence there but all tribes were free to go there to hunt and collect salt which was in abundance. There were many salt springs which attracted many different animals. There were deer, elk, buffalo and just about any kind of animal you could imagine. The settlement of this area by the whites caused great concern and discontent with many tribes.

An occasional flatboat with white settlers would come down the river on their way to Cantukee. My father, who had become village Chief, along with the village Elders, thought it would be in their best interest to try to keep good relations with the whites. So my father along with other men from the village would go out in canoes to greet them and show them the best way to portage around the falls and through the rapids.

Some of the nations in western Pennsylvania renewed their efforts to drive out the settlers in that area and there was much war and carnage in the land. Other's attacked the settlers in northern and western Virginia and Logan was one of these.

Our village remained neutral until a few incidents sent some of our warriors to pick up the war hatchet and join their brothers in attacking the settlers up the Kanawha.

One day three flatboats came into view and my father, with a few men from the village, paddled their canoes out to greet them and offer assistance in portaging the falls and rapids as they had done before.

As the canoes approached the flatboats several white men began shouting obscenities and aimed their muskets at the men in the canoes. One of them fired his rifle and the ball struck the water near my father's canoe.

Not knowing or not caring that my father could understand the words, the white man called my people and all Indians foul names and threatened to kill everyone in the village if any of them came near the flatboats.

Not long after that, two men from our village were out hunting and came upon a group of six or more white men. They approached the group with the intention of asking them what they were doing on the

Ohio side of the river. As they neared the group, the whites opened fire, killing one and severely wounding the other.

The wounded man made it back to the village and told my father what had happened. My father and several warriors went out to retaliate against the white men but could not find them. Their tracking showed the white men had returned to the river and probably went back upstream. They decided not to follow and returned to the village.

At council, it was decided that all of the remaining warriors and boys of fighting age would take up the war hatchet against the settlers. Some of the men chose to go and seek Logan to join up with his war party. Others joined my father to raid up the Kanawha River.

I and my friends were still considered too young to participate and we, along with several others our age, were ordered to stay behind to hunt for and protect the women and old people remaining in the village. We were in our middle teens and considered ourselves warriors. We protested but to no avail.

Logan and his war parties killed a lot of settlers and burned many cabins which prompted the Virginia governor to declare war on all Mingo, Shawnee and Lenape Indians. Unbeknownst to us at the time, this marked the beginning of the end of our peaceful little village.

Jean Lebeau decided to end the trading business and distributed all the rifles, powder and lead he had on hand to the warriors of our village. He declined to join the warriors and gathered the rest of his stock and with the few men who remained in his employ, headed for Canada.

"You will be sorely missed Jean." Cahiktodo said as he helped his old friend pack up supplies. "I hope you fare well up north."

"If we can make it without incident, I should be fine. I have family near Montreal and when I get there, they will help me get settled."

I will be glad to get away from this turmoil and dealing with the British. The West Jersey Trading Company and the men who work for them are fine people, but the rest of them are ignorant, pompous bastards, full of greed and I will never miss dealing with them."

"I am afraid, Cahiktodo, that you and your people's efforts to drive out the settlers will be in vain. The Ohio Company has designs on your lands here and they will stop at nothing to take them. Those men that killed your hunter were working for the Ohio Company. This I heard from very reliable sources. They were sent here to scout out the area. They will return along with many others. You may want to consider moving your people west."

"Jean, I am aware of the settlers wanting the lands of the Ohio Country and in all probabilities they will succeed, but not without cost. If they intend to steal our lands, then they must be prepared to pay the consequence."

"As long as there is the faintest light of hope that we can deter them, we must fight. It is the only way we can hope to preserve our people and our way of life. We will not allow them to wantonly attack us and wipe us from the face of the earth. We will do whatever is necessary to survive as a nation."

"I know you well Cahiktodo. You are a peace loving person. I know how you feel about taking the life of another human being and your tendencies to show mercy. Do you think you can overcome those feelings to attain your goals?"

"I must, I have no choice. I will always be against cruelty and barbarous treatment of prisoners, but I will harbor no misgivings about driving the settlers away from our lands even if it comes to taking the lives of women and children. What must be done, must be done. I will show mercy whenever I can, but not if it would affect the outcome of our efforts."

"Jean, we do have a chance of successfully defending our lands. Cornstalk has urged every man and boy of fighting age in the Shawnee, Delaware and Mingo nations as well as others to take up arms. There are many of us and united we can drive the settlers out."

"There are many whites against you Cahiktodo, and the British have induced the Iroquois and their allies to remain neutral. It will be a tough fight and I hope your people can do as you say. I bid you farewell and wish you good fortune in your efforts."

"Farewell my old friend. I hope you have a safe journey."

Chapter Fourteen

Chingwe paused in his story telling long enough take a drink of water from a gourd. He splashed a little of the water on his face and continued.

Lord Dunmore, the governor of Virginia, declared war on all Mingo, Shawnee and Delaware Indians of the Ohio Country in retaliation for Logan's revenge seeking raids on the settlers of Virginia. He ordered an army of militia to be formed and to march to the Ohio Country to destroy all the Indian villages there.

He split the militia into two forces. One he commanded himself and the other to be commanded by a man named Lewis, Colonel Andrew Lewis.

Dunmore's force would move to Fort Pitt and then travel down the Ohio River. Lewis would lead his force down the Kanawha River to the Ohio where both forces would meet and proceed north to attack the main village of the Shawnee, Chawlagotha.

Cornstalk learned of this plot and ordered runners to all villages to urge the warriors to meet at Chawlagotha. He wanted to sue for peace, but at the urging of the other Chiefs he planned an attack to stop this from happening.

A large force of Shawnee, Delaware, Mingo, Miamis and others gathered there to advance to Tu Endie Wei at the mouth of the Kanawha and do battle with Lewis.

My father, along with all the warriors from our village and the village at Old Town went to Chalawgatha. My friends and I were ordered again to stay at the village to protect it and hunt for the people remaining.

One day several scouts came to the village with a warning.

"You must evacuate the village! Dunmore and his army are now camped at the mouth of the Hockhocking River. They are preparing to march this way to join forces with Lewis at the mouth of the Kanawha. There are many of them and they will destroy every village they come to. The people at Old Town are already preparing to move. You must do the same."

"Will you stay and help us fight them?" I asked.

"No Chingwe, we are on our way to join Cornstalk and attack the army of Lewis when they reach the mouth of the Kanawha. If we can defeat them there we won't have to face the combined forces of both armies."

"You, being the son of the village chief, must take charge here and protect the people. We must go now."

Toti said, "Chingwe, what are we to do? We can't possibly defend the village against such a large force."

"There is only one thing we can do. We must tell the people to gather up their most valuable possessions and head up into the hills to hide until the army passes."

"Toti, you and White Hawk go to the south end of the village and alert the people, I will start at the north side. We must also gather enough boys and old men who can still fight to set up a blocking force if the soldiers try to follow our people up into the hills."

"White Hawk said, "We must tell the people not to build fires when they get into the hills. The smoke will give away their position."

"Good thinking, White Hawk. After we get the people up into the hills and get our blocking force set up, You Toti and I will make our way up river to watch for the soldiers. They may be moving our way now so we must hurry and get the people moving."

As Toti and White Hawked ran off towards the south end of the Village, I stood there just for a moment. It was a sad moment. To think that this village, the only home I had ever known would perhaps be burned to the ground and all the crops destroyed. It felt like a great weight was pressing down upon my shoulders and a tear came to my eye.

"Perhaps they won't burn it." I thought, "I hope they won't destroy my mother's lily field. Maybe they will see the beauty of that place and leave it alone."

I went to my mother and told her what was happening. At first she didn't want to leave. She wanted to go to her lily field with a musket my father had given her to defend it. I managed to talk her into going into the hills with the others.

"Mother, they may not even see the lily field, and if they do, they will see the beauty you created and will not destroy it. Even if they do it harm, there are enough bulbs in the ground that we can dig up and replant them and that won't happen if you are taken by the soldiers. You know father would want you to go to the hills away from the white men and you must do this."

"Are you going to the hills with us?" She asked.

"Toti, White Hawk and I will join you there later. Once we get everyone out of the village we are going to go up river and watch for the white men. We don't want them to come upon us unawares. We will not attempt to fight them. We just want to know where they are and when they will be here. We will watch to see if any of them approach the hiding place. We will have few men and boys ready to fight if necessary to prevent them from attacking should they discover where the people are."

The remaining villagers gathered together and were led by Chingwe and his two friends towards the hills on the other side of the valley. When they got to the foot of the hills Chingwe stopped them and selected one of the older boys in the group.

"Lead them deep into the hills, go north by northwest. Do not go near Old Town for the soldiers will probably go there also. Take them to the place where we gather hickory nuts. There are several caves there that the people can seek shelter in should it rain."

"Do not allow cooking fires made from any wood that will give off a lot of smoke. If you must build a fire, use bark from the Birch tree. Make sure it is dry and use it only long enough to cook."

"Do not fire any muskets. Make sure the younger children stay quiet. We will join you once we have found the army and determined what their intentions are. If the soldiers come this way, we will send a runner to you and hold them off as long as we can. If this happens you must take the people west to the village at Chawlagotha."

"Those that you who are willing to fight and are going to be in the blocking force follow me."

There were only about a dozen old men and young boys old enough to put up a fight against the soldiers should they come this way. We knew they would not be able to resist the soldiers for long, but each was prepared to fight to the death to give the people hiding in the hills as much time as possible to flee to Chawlagotha. We positioned each one where we thought they would be most effective in delaying the soldiers should they come this way.

"Brothers, Toti, White Hawk and myself are now going to move upriver to look for the soldiers. We will be back as soon as we find them and can determine what their intentions are."

My friends and I took off in a trot back towards the river and once we got there turned upstream. We quickly and quietly headed up river expecting any moment to be face to face with the enemy.

We followed along the shore where we could and at times up in the hills overlooking the river. We didn't know if they army would come in boats or if they would be marching on the shore.

At night one of us would always be awake to stand guard as the other two slept. We would move as soon as it was light enough to see where we were going.

We traveled all the way upriver to about a mile from the mouth of the Hockhocking before we saw any sign of the enemy and then it was only a few hunters. We carefully avoided them and made our way to where we could see the main encampment. There were many soldiers there.

That afternoon Toti exclaimed, "Look I think they are starting to move out!"

We watched six canoes, each with three men, push off and paddle across the Ohio. Two men from each canoe got out on the other side of the river and formed a group of about a dozen men there. They began making their way downriver."

At the main encampment we watched as about fifty men lined up and formed ranks. One of the men in the group across the river fired his rifle and the formation on our side of the river started marching downriver towards our hiding place.

"Is this an advance guard?" I thought to myself. "Why aren't the rest of the soldiers forming ranks?"

I told White Hawk to move a little further into the woods, hide himself and keep an eye on the encampment. He was to watch them until midday tomorrow and then hurry downriver and inform us of the whereabouts of the main army.

Bidding White Hawk farewell and wishing him luck Toti and I scurried downriver ahead of the column of soldiers.

That night when the column of soldiers stopped and set up camp, they lit no fires. In the darkness we did notice a small fire on the other side of the river but it was soon extinguished. Toti said they probably built it long enough to cook some meat.

As the column neared the rapids they changed their course and headed for the village at Old Town. Finding no one there, the soldiers began to loot and burn the wigwams, the bark houses and the longhouse.

They set fire to everything they could find, including the cornfields that were just ready for harvesting. The people would go hungry that winter. The air was filled with smoke from their burning. When they finished their business they set up camp.

White Hawk found us that afternoon and said that no more soldiers had come down the river. We thought it strange that they would send such a small force. Small though it was, it was much too large for us to attack. We dreaded the approaching dawn for we knew in our hearts what the soldiers were planning to do.

As dawn broke, Toti hurried to tell the blocking force that the soldiers were approaching and to be on guard.

"I am going back to join Chingwe and White Hawk to see what will happen to our village. If the soldiers come this way, we will be here in plenty of time to join you in holding them off."

Toti rejoined us and we made our way towards Little Buck Town. We found a good hiding place and watched the approaching column.

When the soldiers reached the town, they found it deserted just as they did Old Town. They began to loot and burn here also. They set fire to the longhouse where council meetings were held. A tear came to my eye as I watched them set fire to my father's bark house. They went out and burned our cornfields and I thought to myself, "I hope they stay away from the lily field."

Soon our whole village was ablaze, every wigwam and bark house was burning. Toti pointed across the river and said, "Look Chingwe, they are even burning your grandfather's cabin!"

I looked and saw the smoke billowing up into the air from the trading post. A deep sense of sadness filled my chest. Then it turned to anger and I wanted to go down and kill as many of the soldiers that I could but my friends stopped me.

We watched and waited in anticipation that the soldiers would try to pick up the trail of our people and follow it to destroy them. But to our surprise, they instead cut long poles and laid out the hides they looted. They filled the hides with the booty they stole and tied them to the long poles. They formed their column and began moving back upriver! We followed them for a while and it was plain to see that they were returning to their encampment on the Hockhocking.

My friends and I went back to where we had set up the blocking force and headed for the place were our people were hiding. When we got there a great wail of sadness filled the air as we told the people that our village no longer existed and that all the corn and food stores had been destroyed or looted. They only thing that they hadn't touched was my mother's lily field.

"What are we to do?" asked an old woman with tears streaming down her face. "Where are we to go?"

"There is only one thing we can do now." My mother said, "There is no place to go back to, so we must go to Chawlagotha or one of the villages on the Scioto and join our people there. "

As for myself," I said, "I am going to Tu Endie Wei to join my father and tell him and the warriors that our village is gone. If anyone who is able to fight wants to join me, so be it."

Toti, White Hawk and a couple of older boys said they would go with me. It was sad to see the look on the faces of the old people and hear the crying of the young ones as they packed up what little they had and headed towards the Scioto.

My mother said, "Tell your father to join me at Pekuwe. I will go to the home of his old friend Pucksinwah and I will wait for him there."

My mother embraced each one of us and told us to be careful.

Chapter Fifteen

Chingwe paused for a moment and sighed.

As we headed downriver towards Tu Endie Wei we could faintly hear the sounds of a great fight in the far distance. "We must hurry!" I said, "I wish we had horses!"

We traveled as fast as we could. Sometimes jogging, sometimes walking fast, stopping to rest only when our sides were heaving and the younger boys had trouble keeping up.

Hanging in the air downriver from us, we could see a huge cloud of smoke. Soon we could detect the acrid smell of gunpowder. We could hear the firing ahead of us but as we got closer it dropped off to just a sporadic shot now and then.

"We are too late for the fight!" lamented Toti. "We should have gone overland instead of following the river."

"Too many hills that way Toti, this was the fastest"

As we approached the area across from Tu Endie Wei darkness was beginning to set in. We expected and listened for the victory cries from our warriors across the water. We heard none.

We came across several men carrying wounded warriors and the looks in their faces as they passed made it evident that they had not been victorious.

Soon there were many warriors filtering through the woods heading for the villages on the Scioto. Somehow we managed to find my father and several warriors from our village.

"What are you doing here Chingwe?"

"Father, our village is gone. It was destroyed by men from Dunmore's camp on the Hockhocking. Nothing is left. They even burned the cornfields."

"What about your mother and the others?"

"They are safe father, we made them go into the hills to hide when we found out the soldiers were coming. They are heading to the villages on the Scioto.

The people from Old Town are going there also as that village too was totally destroyed. Mother said to tell you to join her at Pekuwe. She said she would stay at the home of Pucksinwah and meet you there."

"It will be a sad place at the wigwam of Pucksinwah. He was killed in battle today."

"Father," I asked, "What happened across the river?"

"I will tell you when we make camp. For now we must leave this place. Dunmore's army can't be far behind you."

"There is no army behind us father. It was just a small group of about fifty men who came down and destroyed the villages. After they were done with that they went back upriver to Dunmore's camp on the Hockhocking."

"Are you sure of this Chingwe?"

"Yes father, Toti, White Hawk and myself followed them back upriver for a long way. There was no army coming down. The only other men we saw were about a dozen moving downriver on the Virginia side. They burned grandfather's cabin and then we lost track of them after that."

Cahiktodo looked at his warriors. "Did you hear that brothers, no army approaching. What were our scouts thinking! It is too late to go to Cornstalk now with this information. Our warriors are scattered for miles. Come, let's go to the Scioto and find our families."

The group headed towards the Scioto and near dawn we camped to rest. My father, although near complete exhaustion told us of the fight at Tu Endie Wei.

"Lewis" he said, "was camped on the point where the two great rivers meet with about a thousand men. We had but five to six hundred warriors."

"Cornstalk thought that we could surprise them with an early morning frontal attack and with both rivers at their backs we would be able to trap them against the rivers and totally destroy them. This had to be done before Dunmore's army arrived and the two forces combined."

"We built rafts and in the still of the darkness floated across the Ohio a couple miles upriver from Tu Endie Wei. We spread out and began advancing on the enemy at dawn. At first we were successful, pushing the enemy back towards the rivers and killing many."

"Soon the still, morning air was filled with the smoke from all the rifles being fired. It burned the eyes and made it difficult to breathe. In some places you could not see more that a few feet in front of you."

"Some of our warriors threw down their rifles and with tomahawk in hand made their way through the swirling clouds to fight the enemy hand to hand."

"Some who could speak the English language began to call out trying to find the enemy. This did not work well as somc of our warriors were killed by our own men thinking they were the enemy."

"The farther we advanced on the enemy the stronger their return fire became. They were forced to close ranks by the rivers themselves as they were forced to back up to the point. Instead of us trapping them, we made them stronger."

"Cornstalk could be heard moving among the warriors and shouting "Oushi-Cat-o-wee, be strong, be strong!"

"Our scouts had told us that Dunmore was coming downriver to join Lewis and after it became evident that we would not be able to defeat the enemy before dark, Cornstalk, at the urging of the other chiefs, decided to withdraw. He was angry for failing to destroy Lewis's army. He chastised the other chiefs for wanting to quit."

"I felt sorrow for Cornstalk. He didn't want to fight in the first place but agreed to lead us at the urging of those same chiefs that now want to quit and try to make peace."

"I must rest now Chingwe. You and your friends would do well to rest some too. We will sleep until midday then resume our journey to Pekuwe."

When we arrived at Pekuwe we were met by sounds of wailing and mourning. An old woman lamenting the death of Pucksinwah was walking slowly through the village crying "He is no more, He is no more!"

We made our way to the bark house of Pucksinwah where we were met by Chiksika, oldest son of Pucksinwah and his little brother Tecumseh.

"Cahiktodo", Chiksika said, "Your wife Bluebird is safe and she is here. She is with the other women preparing for the burial of my father tomorrow. She told us of the destruction of your village by Dunmore's men. I am sorry to hear of that. Rest assured that you, your family and all the villagers are welcome to stay here as long as you want. You and your men can make temporary shelters until more permanent ones can be erected. You may enter our house for food if you would like. We must be going now for have a lot to do in preparation for father's burial."

"Chiksika," my father replied, "we offer our sympathy on the death of your father. We have suffered a great loss in the destruction of our village but I know the loss of your father weighs heavy on your heart as well as mine. He and I were good friends once. We hunted and fished together. I thank you and your family for your hospitality and taking in my wife."

Chiksika said, "Dunmore and his army are headed towards Chalawgatha. He sent runners ahead to arrange a meeting with Cornstalk and the other chiefs to discuss peace. His runners said that Dunmore ordered Lewis to remain at Tu-Endie-Wei but Lewis has either disobeyed his orders or has not yet received them. Our scouts say that he is preparing to march his men north and burn all the villages he can. After you set up your shelters, you should take your warriors and go south in case Lewis's army comes this way."

"We will do that Chiksika, I will leave my son and his friends to build our shelters and the rest of us will go that way now. Again I thank you for taking us in."

Of course I and my friends were disappointed that we would not be permitted to go with my father.

"Father, haven't we proven we are capable of going with you and fighting the enemy?"

"Yes you have Chingwe, I am proud of you and your friends for protecting the people of our village and getting them safely out of harm's way. But for now, you must stay here, build our shelters and seek out others from our village to help them also."

"If I am not back tomorrow, you must represent our family at the ceremony for Pucksinwah. The time will come soon enough, I'm afraid, that you and your friends will meet the enemy in battle."

My father told his warriors to rest here for a short while and headed off to find my mother.

Cahiktodo found Bluebird working with some other women in preparation of the funeral feast for Puckinswah. She saw him approaching and ran to him.

They embraced and she sobbed, "Oh Cahiktodo, they have destroyed our beautiful village, it is no more. They burned all the corn and even your father's cabin. There is nothing left but ashes. What are we going to do Cahiktodo?"

"I know not yet what our course of action will be. We must wait to see what comes out of this situation before we can council and decide what to do."

"I have been told that we will never be able to go back," cried Bluebird. "Some are saying that the whites will move in and take over the area and we will not be permitted to go back there!"

"They did not harm my lily field so if we cannot re-build our village I want to go there and dig up some of the bulbs."

"Bluebird, do not concern yourself with that right now. If at all possible we will re-build and if not I will take you there to get your lily bulbs."

"You would have been proud of your son Cahiktodo. He took charge and made sure all of the villagers were moved to safety. He and his friends even went to scout out the enemy and had the foresight to make plans to stop them from following us to our hiding place."

"I am proud of him Bluebird, but I am also afraid for him. I fear the future will be bleak for all the Indians."

"If only we had known that Dunmore was not coming downriver to reinforce Lewis! We could have pressed our attack and probably would have succeeded in destroying the army at Tu-Endie-Wei. Then it would have been Dunmore instead of us seeking peace and giving concessions."

"I must go now Bluebird. My men are waiting. We are going south to watch for Lewis's army. It is said that they are on their way to attack us against Dunmore's wishes. We will do whatever it takes to stop them. Chingwe and his friends are building shelters for us. You and I will be together again soon."

They embraced again and Cahiktodo rushed off to join his warriors.

Chapter Sixteen

Chingwe sent Gray Squirrel to fetch his pipe and tobacco pouch from the shelter.

"Hurry Squirrel!" Dark Sky shouted, "I want to hear more!"

Gray Squirrel scurried to the shelter and grabbed his grandfather's pipe and pouch. He ran back to the fire and handed them to his grandfather. Chingwe took his time filling his pipe and lighting it as the children waited in anticipation.

"Where was I?" Grandfather asked.

"You were telling us of Cahiktodo and his warriors going to stop Lewis and his army from attacking Pekuwe"

Lewis and his army did burn a few small villages on their advance up the Scioto but changed their course and headed to Chawlagotha to meet up with Dunmore's army. Dunmore had arrived at Chawlagotha and was preparing to hold council with Cornstalk and the other chiefs to discuss peace. I heard that when Lewis arrived he and Dunmore had a heated argument. Lewis wanted to destroy all the villages, but Dunmore wanted peace.

After we buried Pucksinwah, my father allowed us to accompany him and his warriors to Chawlagotha. It was the last time that I saw Logan.

Near the village, a site was chosen to hold peace talks. There were many soldiers and warriors gathered there and the principle chiefs and the white officers gathered under the shade of an enormous elm tree on Sippo Creek.

My friends and I positioned ourselves as close to this spot as we could get so we could hear what was being said. First the white men spoke and then each chief stood and presented their concerns.

All but one spoke for peace. When it was Logan's turn to speak he stood defiantly in front of the white officers and I will always remember the words he spoke.

"I appeal to any white man to say, if ever he entered Logan's cabin hungry, and he gave him not meat. If ever he came cold and naked, and he clothed him not. During the course of the last long and bloody war, Logan remained idle in his cabin, an advocate for peace."

"Such was my love for the whites, that my countrymen pointed as they passed, and said, Logan is the friend of the white men. I have even thought to live with you but for the injuries of one man. Colonel Cresap who, the last spring, in cold blood, and unprovoked, murdered all the relations of Logan, not sparing even my women and children. There runs not a drop of my blood in the veins of any living creature. This has called on me for revenge. I have sought it, I have killed many, I have fully glutted my vengeance."

"For my country, I rejoice at the beams of peace. But do not harbor a thought that mine is the joy of fear. Logan never felt fear. He will not turn on his heel to save his life. Who is there to mourn for Logan? Not one."

In his talk, Logan said that it was a Colonel Cresap that murdered his family. It was actually Greathouse who did this terrible thing but Logan always felt it was done at Cresap's urging.

An agreement was reached and peace was declared but at a cost. We had to give up our right to hunt in Cantukee and had to agree that the Spaylawetheepi would be the boundary between us and the British Colonists. We would no longer be permitted to go beyond the river. Some of our people were outraged at this but all finally agreed to the terms of the treaty.

After the armies left, my father called for a council to include the village chief of Old Town, their elders and the elders of Quenolapay Ohtenatit to decide whether to go back and re-build the villages or not. It was decided that with the Cantukee lands now open for settlement as well as the lands across the river it would not be a wise thing to do. The river would be filled with white settlers moving into these areas and we would be placing ourselves in jeopardy of further death and destruction.

The treaty said that the British government would not allow white settlers to move into the lands north of the river but that promise rang hollow to the ears of the people. They had witnessed the men from the Ohio Company surveying near the villages and in their hearts knew it would be just a matter of time before the whites would begin settling in their lands.

The Lenape among us decided they would travel east to one of the Delaware villages on the Muskingum. The Shawnee would settle in Pekuwe and Chawlagotha.

There was a great sadness in the hearts of all the people when this decision was reached. My friend Toti, a Delaware, did not want to go to the Muskingum and asked his father if he could stay with us. His father was reluctant at first but after speaking with my father he allowed Toti to stay.

Our village of Little Buck Town, once so peaceful and serene was never to be again. My mother, who was Lenape by birth, was extremely saddened. Her mother and father would be moving to the Muskingum and she would never be able take care of her lily field again.

"Bluebird, as soon as I can, I will take you back to your lily field to get bulbs. You can plant another lily filed here."

"Cahiktodo, I am saddened that we will not be going back to our village to live. I wanted so much to be buried there with our ancestors. The lily field was a memorial to them, now it will belong to the whites and they will not appreciate the beauty and the meaning behind it. I will go and collect bulbs and I will create another lily field, but it won't be the same. I already miss the sound of the falls."

"Why can't all the white people be like our friend Anne and her husband in Philadelphia? Why do they want to drive us from our villages and destroy our way of life? Why...why?"

"I cannot answer that Bluebird. I know there are no finer people that Joseph and Anne Miller. But I believe that the white men in general are driven by greed and will not stop at anything to get what they want. It is that type of people that I hate. Our way of life means nothing to them."

"Sometimes I wish I could remove this tattoo from my arm and the white blood from my veins."

"I fear that we are soon to witness a flooding of white people coming into our country and I don't know if we will be able to stem the flood or not. I know that the Shawnee alone cannot do it. Only if the nations could put aside their differences for a while and become one, would we have a chance of pushing the white men back to the east."

Not long after the battle at Tu Endie Wei, there was a great fight between the British and their colonists. The colonists began calling themselves Americans. We called them Shemanese or Long Knives.

At first most of the Shawnee and Delaware chiefs wanted to be neutral. Others wanted to join the

British effort. Cornstalk was one of the main advocates for peace and neutrality. He was determined to keep his promises made with Dunmore and even traveled to the fort the Shemanese had built at Tu Endie Wei to warn them that some of the Indians were ready to join the British.

In a treacherous act, the Shemanese commander made Cornstalk and those with him prisoners and were going to hold them for ransom!

A white soldier was killed by a Shawnee warrior outside the fort one day and those within the fort brutally murdered Cornstalk, his son Elinipsico and two other Shawnee.

This act infuriated the Shawnee and Lenape. It ended any chance of remaining neutral.

It was during this time that I and my friends were finally allowed to go on a war party with my father.

Chapter Seventeen

Cahiktodo stood in front of his son and his young friends.

"Chingwe, Toti and White Hawk, today you will be going on your first war party. I must tell you this is not a game like you used to play in the woods near our village. You will be expected to act like men and warriors. You must obey all orders without question. You will experience things that will affect you the rest of your lives. "

"Undoubtedly you will have to take the life of another human being. Do not hesitate in doing this. It is of the utmost importance that we make the whites understand that this is our land, our way of life and that we will protect it by any means necessary."

"You will experience fear and hatred. You may experience the death of a friend or relative. Turn these emotions into righteous anger and use them to feed your intensity in battle."

"You will see the side of some of your friends and relatives that you never saw before. Their cruelty may shock you. Do not judge them for their actions for we are facing determined enemies who have it in their hearts to steal our lands and destroy our way of life. We must do whatever necessary to deter them from their quest."

"I don't want you to think that showing mercy and abstaining from cruelty is a weakness. It is not. It is a strength, but you must learn when and when not to use them. Listen to the thoughts that come to you from your heart. Judgment comes from the mind, emotions come from the heart. You must be wise enough to quickly determine which is best for the situation you are in."

"Now, go and rest, we are leaving at day break."

My friends and I were up well before daybreak. By the light of a fire we painted our faces for war. We had been given horses to ride and we painted them also.

When the sun came up, we ate a little and mounted our horses. We joined the rest of the warriors and felt so proud as we rode through the village. There were a dozen of us. The people lined up and wished us well as we passed. We were finally going to fight and prove our manhood.

We traveled to the Spaylawetheepi and followed it upriver for about a mile and a half past Fort Randolph. We located some canoes that were hidden there and crossed the Spaylawetheepi. We moved overland on foot to the Kanawha a mile or so above the fort.

We located two cabins that the whites had built on the banks of the Kanawha. We counted 4 men, two young boys, two women and a small girl. They had already begun to cut down the trees along the river and had begun clearing an area to plant crops.

We moved upriver from the cabins, settled in for the night and made plans for attack the next morning. My father, two other warriors Palawi and Okowellos, my friends and I hid ourselves in the brush between the cabins and the field the whites had been clearing. The others positioned themselves around the cabins. As the sun came up, the whites came out of their cabins and the men and two young boys made their way to the fields.

We watched and waited for what seemed an eternity. Suddenly the air was filled with the sounds of muskets being fired back at the cabins. Our warriors had begun their attack. We could hear the women screaming and the war whoops of our warriors.

The men and boys in the field threw down their tools and grabbed their rifles. They began to run towards to cabin, right in our direction. We opened fire with our rifles and two of the men and one of the young boys went down.

Okowellos, in hiding next to us let out a scream and rushed out of the brush with tomahawk in hand. He streaked towards one of the standing white men who raised his rifle and brought down Okowellos with a shot in the chest.

My father then broke from cover and brought down that white man with a tomahawk blow to the head. The other white man and boy fired their muskets at my father but both missed.

My friends and I charged out of the brush towards them but my father and Palawi were already there. We watched as they fought.

The young boy went down quickly as Palawi dodged his swinging musket and struck the boy with his tomahawk in the back of the head.

My father grappled with the white man who was much bigger than him. The white man had a knife in his hand and my father held a tomahawk. Each had hold of the other's wrist as they struggled. My father jerked his knee up into the white man's groin and as he doubled over he finished him with a blow from his tomahawk.

Palawi began screaming and drawing his knife from its sheath, he removed the scalp from the young boy he had just killed. He then moved over to the fallen man and removed his scalp also. He stuffed the scalps into his pouch and moved over to the others. He scalped them as well.

My father had walked over to the fallen Okowellos and finding him dead, knelt down beside the body and began removing his shot pouch, powder horn and other things.

My friends and I were standing there looking at my father and the dead Okowellos, we were visibly shaken and my father looked up at us and said, "Help me carry him to the river."

Carrying Okowellos towards the cabins I saw one of the warriors there holding up the scalp of a woman. He was covered with blood.

Three of them were inside the cabins looking for plunder and the other two were standing on the river bank looking out into the water. One of them raised his rifle and fired a shot.

As we approached the two on the bank, I saw what the warrior was firing at. The other woman and the young girl had dove into the Kanawha to escape us and were clinging to a floating log just about midway into the river. The warrior was just finishing reloading and raised his rifle to shoot again when my father said, "Stop, let them go."

The warrior turned on my father and said, "No, we must kill them before they reach the safety of the fort!"

He started to raise his rifle again and my father grabbed the barrel and jerked it from his hand.

"I said let them go! The soldiers from the fort surly heard the firing of our rifles and will be coming this way soon. We have to take care of the body of Okowellos, set fire to these cabins and leave this place before they get here."

He turned away from the warrior and tossed the rifle to me.

This angered the warrior even more and he yelled, "You are a woman Cahiktodo, you show too much mercy, we must kill all of the white settlers! You are not fit to lead us, perhaps I should......."

In a flash, like the movement of a cat, my father had the warrior on his back on the ground and his knife at his throat.

"I am the leader of this war party and you will do as you are told. If you do not, you may never see Pekuwe again! Now get up and help us, or get up and go back to the village now!"

We found a large blanket in one of the cabins and placed the body of our fallen warrior into it. We put some rocks in with him and tied the blanket up. We carried him out into the river and let him sink beneath the waters of the Kanawha. He will be greatly missed back at Pekuwe. He left behind a wife and two young sons.

We had planned to go on up the Kanawha and attack a few more cabins, but my father decided to return to the village. We had much loot that we got from these cabins. Iron skillets, a Dutch oven, blankets, lead, powder, an axe and other tools.

We set fire to the cabins, bundled up the goods and headed back towards our canoes we had hidden on the Spaylawetheepi.

We crossed the river and found our horses we had hobbled. We tied most of the goods on the horse of Okowellos and started our journey back to Pekuwe. It was a silent journey. No one did much talking.

When we arrived back at Pekuwe, the people greeted us and the warriors with the scalps rode through the village whooping and displaying their trophies.

My father dismounted and walked directly to the wigwam of Okowellos to let his wife know that he would not be returning. A wail of despair erupted from the wigwam and my father exited with a sad look on his face. He motioned for me to follow him and we went to our wigwam.

My mother embraced both of us and told us how glad she was that we returned safely. She prepared a fine meal for us and after we ate my father told her what had happened on the raid."

The next morning a visitor appeared. It was Simon Girty, the man my father had met long ago at Fort Pitt.

"Simon, it's good to see you." My father greeted his old friend with a bear hug.

"I am happy to see you too Cahiktodo and Bluebird, just look at you. Just as pretty as you ever was!"

My mother covered her mouth with her hand and looked down. She was embarrassed by his statement. When Simon offered his hand she took it and he smiled at her.

He turned to me and said, "Is this your son Cahiktodo? He looks a lot like you."

"Yes, this is Chingwe. He has just returned from his first war party. He will be a good warrior. Come, let's go inside and sit. Bluebird will make us something good to eat."

We entered the wigwam and sat down.

"Tell me Simon", my father said. "What brings you to Pekuwe?"

"I just came to visit. I was going to visit you and Bluebird at Little Buck Town but I learned that Dunmore's men had destroyed it. I tried to persuade my Seneca brothers to join in the fight against Dunmore but they refused to consider it."

"When the fighting between the colonists and the British broke out I joined up with the Colonials for a while but I soon realized the Colonial whites were just as bad if not worse than the British."

"I figured that Indians would have a better chance negotiating with the British rather than the land hungry colonists so I took up with them and am now serving as an interpreter again."

"Cahiktodo, I want to tell you something. I am getting tired of fighting. I don't think anyone will be able to stop the flow of whites into our lands. After his fight is over I am going up north to Canada. I will try to live out my life in peace. You and your family are welcome to go with me if you'd like."

"As for now though, I am obligated to try to keep the ties of the Indian allies with the British and I will continue to lead war parties against the settlers but when this is over, I am going north, I have had enough."

"I have seen some terrible things Cahiktodo. Captives made to run the gauntlet and being burned at the stake! It makes me sick to think that one human being can treat another one that way. These were my own Seneca brothers!"

"It also sickens me that the whites feel they can torture and butcher Indians then call the Indians savages for their treatment of whites, as if their forms of torture and butchery are not as bad as the Indians. I tell you, I am tired of it all."

"Tomorrow I am going into council with Shawnee, Delaware, Mingo and Miami chieftains to tell them of the latest British proposals and support."

"Between you and me Cahiktodo, I don't think the British will keep the promises they make. They never did in the past. I don't know why the British think the Indians will believe them now, but it is my job to make them believe and this also sickens me."

Bluebird entered with a platter of meat.

"Bluebird, those flowers you carted from Philadelphia, did you ever get them planted?"

"Yes I did, Simon. With the help of my son and his friends we created a beautiful field of lilies that rivaled the gardens of Philadelphia. I wish you could have seen it."

"Me too Bluebird. I wish I could have made a visit to your village before it was destroyed."

"The village was destroyed, but the lily field is still there. Cahiktodo and I will soon journey there to get some bulbs. I will make another lily field near here."

"And it will be just as beautiful as the one she created on the river." Cahiktodo added.

After we ate my father and Simon went for a walk and my mother told me again of her trip to Philadelphia. It was good to see her smile as she recounted the story of her journey and the time she spent with her friend Anne in the lily garden there.

That evening my father and I went for a walk along the banks of the Scioto.

"My son, now you know that making war is not a game. There is always sadness and sorrow on one side or the other, sometimes both. Tell me your thoughts."

"Father, I hope you don't think I am not made to be a warrior, but I have sorrow for the deaths of those white people. I cannot forget the look of terror in the eyes of that woman and her little girl out in that river."

"I have mixed feelings of sorrow and anger for that man that killed Okowellos."

"Okowellos killed himself." Cahiktodo said. "He made a mistake and paid for it with his life. He should not have charged the man until the man had fired his rifle. Okowellos made poor judgment. He should have waited until the man's rifle was empty."

"As for feeling sorry for those we killed, I too harbor these feelings. I especially hate the killing of women and children. But such things are necessary at times. It upsets me that some of my own people revel in such things and celebrate like they have been victorious over some great warrior."

"There are acts of cruelty on both sides my son. Remember what the whites did to Logan's family?"

"Will it ever stop father?"

"Chingwe, I am afraid that peace between the nations and the whites will not be seen in our life time. There is too much difference in the way of life for both sides to live peacefully side by side. We will probably be fighting the whites for years to come."

"They are controlled by greed. They will stop at nothing to take all the lands of the Indians and force us to become totally dependent on them. They desire to rule us rather than live with us."

"They are deceitful by nature and cannot even live amongst themselves without letting their greed control them. They use the nations to help them gain what their greed dictates. It has always been that way."

"Now that the British are fighting those that call themselves Americans and the nations are being torn apart again. Both sides ply the Indians with their trade goods and promises that they never intend to keep. As a result, the Indians always end up being the losers."

"If only the Indian nations would come together as one would we have a real chance of driving the whites from our lands. But I don't think that will ever happen."

"Can you imagine the Six Nations of the Iroquois joining forces with all of the Algonquin speaking nations? There would be so many warriors that the whites would be scrambling to the east coast to board ships and return to England."

"The Indian tribes of this land hold to many grudges against each other and are too stubborn to forgive each other for past differences and conflicts to ever become one. The whites count on this. They know how to turn one tribe against another. Plus the white man's greed has infected the leaders of a lot of nations. Tribal unification is just a dream."

[illegible] I am afraid [illegible] peace between the [illegible] and the whites will not be seen in our life[illegible]. There is too much difference in the way of life [illegible] to live peacefully side by side. [illegible] will [illegible] for quite some time.

They are controlled by Greed. They will stop at nothing [illegible] lands of my Indians and [illegible] to become totally dependent on them [illegible] rather than [illegible].

They are [illegible] their rights [illegible] without [illegible] greed [illegible]. They [illegible] to [illegible] what their greed dictates. [illegible]

Now that the British are signing trade that can [illegible] the nations [illegible] Indians with their trade goods [illegible]. As a result the Indians are [illegible].

If only the Indian nations would come together as one [illegible] capable of driving the whites from our lands. But I don't think that will ever happen.

[illegible] all of the [illegible] speaking [illegible] in [illegible] to England.

The Indian tribes [illegible] against each other and are too stubborn to [illegible] each other. [illegible] differences and conflicts [illegible]. The whites [illegible]. They know how to [illegible] against [illegible]. [illegible] great [illegible] nations. [illegible] is just a dream.

Chapter Eighteen

"Grandfather", Dark Sky said to Chingwe, "Do you think there will ever be peace in my life time? Will we ever be able to go back and live at Quenolapay Ohtenatit?"

"There will never be an Indian village at Little Buck Town ever again. The whites control the area now and they will never give it up and as far as peace in your life time, Dark Sky, it may come, but only fleetingly. Like my father said, there is too much difference in our ways of life for peace to last long."

"Why did they kill Cornstalk?" Gray Squirrel asked.

"I don't know their reasoning Gray Squirrel, perhaps they feared him."

"After Cornstalk was murdered," continued Chingwe, "Black Fish became principle chief of the Shawnee. He sought revenge by leading war parties up the Kanawha River and also in parts of Pennsylvania."

That was the year the Shemanese called the "Year of the bloody sevens. It was their year 1777.

My father's friend Simon Girty managed to line up many tribes to join the British in their fight against the Shemanese. They were the Shawnee, Delaware, Mingo, Wyandot, Kickapoo, Ottawa, Ojibwa, Potawatomis, Miami, Sauk, Fox, Chickamauga and Mascoutons. Many Shemanese settlements and cabins were attacked and destroyed.

My father and I were in many war parties. We went up the Kanawha, over to the Cantukee lands, across the river into Virginia. We carried out attacks in our own Ohio country and parts of Pennsylvania.

During this time an army of at least three hundred mounted Shemanese from the Cantukee lands attacked Chawlagotha and burned it. They also burned all the cornfields around it and killed Black Fish.

The Shawnee decided to move all the villages along the Scioto further north to better protect them. That year Simon Girty led a war party against the Shemanese fort called Fort Laurens and killed many.

At that time many people from the village of Pekuwe grew tired of fighting and went west to settle in Louisiana.

I took a wife about this time. She was the daughter of a Pekuwe warrior who left for Louisiana. Her name was Kanti, One who sings. She was your grandmother. She was a beautiful woman and I fell in love with her the first time I saw her. When her father agreed to allow her to become my woman, and we joined in the Wedding Dance, it was the happiest time of my life.

Our first child was your uncle, Ahanu, He Laughs. He was followed by your father Pajackok, Thunder, and then came little Nuttah, My Heart. Little Nuttah was a beautiful child and very inquisitive. She loved to play with the village dogs and they took to her like she was their leader. She would sometimes dress them up in other animal skins and even the meanest dogs would allow her to do this. She caught the white man's fever before she reached womanhood and her death nearly broke my heart.

Your father Pajackok is a very brave warrior. As a child he was always one of the leaders in the games the young men played. He also has inherited the dislike of the senseless slaughter of women and children as well as the torture of captives. I hope these traits pass down to you boys as well. Remember cruelty is not a sign of braveness.

"Blue Feather, you look so much like your mother. Pajackok took her as his wife just after his seventeenth summer. Oota Dabun, The Star, I have met no woman who can cook like her. You are very close to being as good as she Blue Feather and I would say with a little practice you will some day surpass her."

"Did Bluebird ever get to go back to her lily field? Blue Feather asked. Did she ever get to plant another one?"

A look of sadness came over Chingwe's face.

"I will tell you of that later." He said. Right now let us prepare for our evening meal. First thing in the morning I will go alone to visit with my white friend who now has settled near the field to see if he will permit us to go there."

"He is a white man grandfather? Will he allow us? How did you ever make friends with a white man?" Dark Sky asked.

"I will tell you later this evening," Answered Chingwe, "for now let's go see if we can catch another fish or two for supper."

Chingwe and the two boys went to the river and Blue Feather sat about preparing other things to go with the fish. It wasn't long before Chingwe and the boys returned with not just two fish, but six huge catfish.

They cleaned the fish and presented the filets to Blue Feather who soon had them sizzling in the huge iron skillet that her mother had sent with her.

The boys stood over the fire watching and smelling the fish frying in the skillet and their mouths watered as they anticipated the meal they were soon going to enjoy.

After the meal, Chingwe sat down by the fire and said, "After the Shemanese defeated the British and formed their own Nation, things got worse and worse for the Indians living in the Ohio Country. The whites built a settlement at the mouth of the

Muskingum and called it Marietta. After that settlement was established, the whites poured into our lands."

There had been many battles fought during the years following Tu Endie Wei. Bad things were committed by both sides. The whites murdered almost a hundred Delaware in the village of Gnadenhutten. These were peaceful Indians who had converted to their Christianity. They were murdered by militia from Pennsylvania. This caused the Lenape nation to seek revenge.

Later that year the Shemanese set out to destroy the villages in the Sandusky area. They were led by a Shemanese commander named Crawford.

My father's friend Simon Girty led a war party to intercept them. Simon's force succeeded in defeating the invaders and capturing Crawford. Crawford was turned over to the Delaware and they burned him at the stake.

Girty later told my father that he knew Crawford from the time he worked as an interpreter at Fort Pitt. He bore no personal hatred for the man and once they were friends so to speak.

Crawford begged Girty to intervene on his behalf but Girty could not do it. As disgusted with this type of torture as he was, he could not risk placing himself and his leadership in jeopardy by defending this enemy of the Delaware.

He told my father that during the burning, he almost pulled a pistol to end Crawford's suffering as Crawford kept calling his name, but thought better of it when he noticed he was being watched by several warriors.

Simon Girty led many raids. After the defeat of Crawford's army he led us on a raid into the Cantukee lands. We attacked the settlers at Bryant's Station there. The Shemanese militia pursued us and Girty set up an ambush for them and we killed over sixty of their soldiers and captured many more.

Girty was a white man by birth but he was a Seneca by adoption. He was well respected by all the Indian Nations.

The white men hated him and called him a renegade. In truth he was just a man who followed his heart. He knew what the intentions of the British were from the beginning and the Shemanese intentions in the end. He was solely for justice for the Indians and decided to follow his principles and fight for their rights. He is living in Canada now, just like he told my father.

The Indians of the Ohio Country met with the Shemanese at their fort called Fort Greenville and most agreed to sign a peace treaty setting yet again the boundaries between the Indian lands and the white settlers.

Of course the white settlers ignored these boundaries and continued to encroach upon Indian Territory. The Indians who signed the treaty were forced to sell some of their lands to the Shemanese government.

This infuriated Tecumseh, son of Pucksinwah. He said, "No tribe has the right to sell, even to each other, much less to strangers.... Sell a country! Why not sell the air, the great sea, as well as the earth? Didn't the Great Spirit make them all for the use of his children? The only way to stop this evil is for the red man to unite in claiming a common and equal right in the land, as it was first, and should be now, for it was never divided."

Pucksinwah's son Tecumseh had lost his brother Chiksika in battle. Tecumseh was a brilliant man and a gifted speaker who could converse, read and write in English as well as any white man.

He understood that the white tide of settlers could never be turned unless the Indian nations put aside their differences and joined as one in defending their lands from white encroachment.

He enlisted the help of one of his younger brothers named Lalawethika to help him unite all the tribes. Tecumseh met resistance from many so called “peace Chiefs” of the tribes. Including his own chief Black Hoof, now principal chief of the Shawnee nation. He had to work hard to convince the tribes to unite with him.

Lalawethika in the beginning was not much of an influence on anybody. He had taken to the white man’s whisky and it began to control his life.

Once, while in an alcoholic stupor, he claimed to have had a vision and after that he gave up alcohol and became a religious leader. He preached that white people were the children of the serpent, the great evil spirit of the world and that his people should not use anything made by the white men, including foods, clothing, manufactured goods and especially alcohol.

Lalawethika, He who makes a loud noise, changed his name to Tenskatawa or The Open Door. He managed to gather a large following and he and Tecumseh went to where the Tippecanoe and Wabash rivers meet. They formed a large village there and named it Prophetstown.

Tecumseh travelled great distances to meet with the leaders of other tribes and persuade them to ally their warriors with his and attack the whites in one swift move as a united force.

The time of the attack would be revealed to them when Tecumseh felt all the forces were prepared and in place. He even got the British to promise to support his forces when the time was right.

Tecumseh selected a few warriors from Prophetstown, including myself to accompany him south to meet with the chiefs of the Creek nation. Before we left he instructed his brother Tenskatawa not to have anything to do with the enemy and to avoid any and all confrontations with them for he knew the time was not right for any type of conflict. Any failure would destroy his plans to unite the tribes.

While we were gone the Shemanese government ordered their commander, William Henry Harrison, to put an end to all threats of Indian hostilities. Harrison moved his forces towards Prophetstown and built a fort there which he named Fort Harrison after himself. He sent spies into Prophetstown and discovered that Tecumseh had assembled nearly three thousand warriors from different tribes.

In the late fall, Harrison moved more than a thousand of his soldiers to Prophetstown and encamped them on the Tippecanoe River. He was trying to goad The Prophet into a fight. It worked.

Disregarding the instructions from his brother Tecumseh, Tenskwatawa ordered the warriors to attack the Shemanese camp promising that they would be victorious and none of them would be killed for he would "cast a spell" making the bullets of the white men bounce off their bodies. His spell would also confuse the white men and make them kill each other.

The warriors attacked and as Tenskwatawa stood on a hill overlooking the battle. He began chanting to make his spell work. His efforts to cast the spell failed as did the warriors. They suddenly realized the white men's bullets were killing them and it looked as if they had no intentions of killing each other.

Harrison's soldiers drove the warriors back, entered Prophetstown and burned it to the ground."

As we were returning from our journey in the south, we heard what had happened and Tecumseh was furious. When we arrived at what was left of Prophetstown he nearly killed his brother. He stripped him of all authority and banished him to Canada.

Right after that the British and Americans began to fight each other again. The British made Tecumseh a General in their army.

We fought many battles and always hoped that Tecumseh's dream would someday come true. But that dream ended at the Battle of the Thames. Tecumseh was killed there and our hopes of a united Indian nation died with him.

I returned to Kanti and built a cabin in the style of the white men on the Scioto near where the old village of Chawlagotha once stood.

Soon white people began building cabins nearby. Some were friendly, some were not. We were forced to move.

Now, upon the completion of our visit here, we will all head west to Missouri. We cannot live there on the Scioto any longer. Just like the little village here, where I was born, everything is gone. Life can never be the way it was.

"Grandfather," Said Blue Feather, What about Bluebird and the lily field? Did she ever get to return here?

"How did you make friends with the white men who are living here now? Added Dark Sky.

"I will tell you these things now so you can understand why I wanted to bring you here to see where I was born and the memories this place invokes."

Chapter Nineteen

"Children," Chingwe said, "what I am about to tell you now, comes from my heart. I did not witness these events, but I know they happened. After many, many hours of meditation the spirits revealed to me what I am about to say."

Cahiktodo had promised Bluebird that he would someday take her back to the old village to see if she could collect some of the bulbs from the beautiful field of lilies she had created. That day came. It was just after the destruction of Old Chawlagotha and the village of Peckuwe was fading away as a lot of the people there decided to head west to get away from the encroaching whites.

Cahiktado warned Bluebird, "There are probably white people living there now. The field may have been destroyed. We are taking a chance going back there. Do you really want to go?"

"Of course I do, Cahiktodo. I must see the field once more and bring back some of Anne's flowers for our people to see and enjoy. I promise to be very careful and stay just long enough to dig up some bulbs to bring back."

"All right, we will leave in the morning. Chingwe will not be able to go with us as he is going on a war party in the morning. Say your goodbye to him early so you both can get plenty of rest. I told Chingwe we would be back in a few days."

The next morning they travelled cross country to the Scioto River. They climbed into an old dugout canoe that had been left in a hiding place near the river. They paddled out into the current and let it slowly take them southward. They entered the Ohio River at the mouth and here they had to paddle against the current to take them upriver towards their old village site.

As they paddled upriver on the Ohio they encountered several flatboats loaded with settlers heading towards the Cantukee lands. When they saw them they beached their canoe and hid in the woods.

They saw quite a few cabins on the Virginia side of the river and a few here and there on the Ohio side.

As they neared the falls they pulled their canoe ashore near the big rock where Cahiktodo and his son Chingwe used to play as children. They hid the canoe there and made their way toward the village, being careful to stay hidden and make as little noise as possible.

When the site of the old village came into view they were dismayed to see several cabins being built by white people. None had been completed yet. It looked as though they had been there only a short while. Smoke from their fires drifted up into the air.

They made their way around the settlers along the river and were headed above the falls when they saw another cabin near the place where Bluebird had created her lily field. This cabin had been there for some time. There was corn growing in a field next to the cabin and what looked like a well tended garden. They saw horses, cows and several pigs enclosed in a fence made of split rails.

Bluebird's heart was pounding in her chest as they neared the lily field. She couldn't believe her eyes. The field was covered with the lilies she had planted and was ablaze with all the colors of the rainbow.

She ran out into the field and twirled around taking in as much of the beauty as she could. Much to the consternation of Cahiktodo. He was warily watching for any sign of white men approaching.

After a while, Bluebird began digging up bulbs and placing them in her baskets.

Cahiktodo said, "Bluebird, stay low while you are digging and be aware of what is going on around you. If you see the approach of anyone, race to the woods and find a hiding place. I am going down to the river above the falls and see if I can tell what is going on with those white men. Promise me you will be alert. I will be back for you shortly."

"I will Cahiktodo, and you promise you will be careful too. Don't let those white men see you. I love you Cahiktodo."

"And I love you Bluebird."

Cahiktodo made his way to the river bank and began slowly moving downriver towards the falls. He could hear the distant talking, the laughter and the sounds of the men working on their cabins. He wanted to see if he could make out the spot where his wigwam once stood. So much had changed.

He laid down his rifle and was kneeling down in the brush studying the white men when he heard a noise behind him. Turning he saw a flash of white. A huge buck deer stepped out of the trees and was making its way down towards the river to drink. It was as white as winter snow and had eyes that were as red as coals in a fire.

Startled at first, Cahiktodo stood up expecting the deer to bolt into the woods. Instead the dear stopped and stared at Cahiktodo. In that instant, the dream Cahiktodo had years ago in Philadelphia, came back to him. Fear rose in his throat. He felt as though he should run, but was afraid he would come to the attention of the white men if he did.

The deer began snorting and stamping his hooves. Cahiktodo stood there and stared at the deer, anticipating a charge at any second. He pulled the tomahawk from his belt.

Suddenly the air was filled with the most hideous scream that Cahiktodo had ever heard. It sounded like the screaming of a wildcat but twice as loud and rose to a high pitch and seemed to echo through the surrounding hills. The deer bolted at this sound and bounded back into the woods. It suddenly dawned on Cahiktodo what the sound was.

"Wetzel!" He thought, "Bluebird!"

Grabbing his rifle he sprang into the woods towards the lily field.

"Bluebird!" he shouted as he tore through the underbrush, "Bluebird!"

"There was a noise like the cracking of thunder as somewhere in the woods ahead of him a rifle went off. He heard the sound of the ball whizzing through the air towards him and felt it smack into his chest just below his breast.

The force of the ball knocked him to the ground. The ball made a hole about the size of a robin's egg in his chest but in his back, where it exited, there was a hole the size of a robin's nest.

Cahiktodo knew it was a death wound and that he only had a short time to live. Bleeding profusely, he painfully pulled himself across the ground and sat with his back against the trunk of a maple tree.

He closed his eyes and feigned death as his assailant approached him. He could hear him shuffling through the leaves on the forest floor. He could smell the stench of his body as the white man reached down and grabbed him by his hair.

With all the strength he could muster, Cahiktodo swung his tomahawk at the white man's head. The white man easily dodged the blow and struck Cahiktodo in the face with his fist.

Cahiktodo looked up at the white man towering over him. He was dressed in greasy buckskin covered with blood. His hair was long and greasy, almost down to his waist.

Near death, Cahiktodo attempted to stand and muster one more swing. Wetzel stood and watched as Cahiktodo struggled to his feet and leaned back against the tree for support. Wetzel then thrust his knife deep into Cahiktodo's heart.

Wetzel took Cahiktodo's scalp and pushed it into a pouch on his belt. In the pouch was another scalp, that of a woman.

Wetzel grabbed Cahiktodo's legs and drug him down towards the river where he cut all the clothes off the body and unceremoniously kicked the lifeless Cahiktodo into the water.

He stood and watched as the slowly sinking body of Cahiktodo was drawn by the current out into the river. The water swirled red with Cahiktodo's blood.

Leaning back his head, Wetzel let out another scream that reverberated through the hills, across the river and downstream.

The men who had been working on their cabins had dropped their tools and grabbed their rifles. They stood staring into the woods. Eyes wide with terror, they expected a horde of Indians to come charging out of the woods at any second.

Chapter Twenty

The children were crying now and a tear or two streamed down Chingwe's face as he continued.

That is what the spirits told me.

When I returned from that war party, my mother and father were not there. I waited for a few days and was about to go search for them when I had to go and fight again.

Weeks passed, then months with no word from my mother and father. It was not until after the Battle of the Thames that I got the opportunity to go and see if I could find out what happened to Cahiktodo and Bluebird. Leaving my family on the Scioto I set out alone to the lily field.

When I got there, I saw quite a few cabins where the old village used to be. It was like a village again, except this time it was white people living there.

I made my way to the lily field and was surprised to see it in full bloom. The white people had left it alone. The lilies had spread and covered nearly every inch of the field.

I was standing there taking in the beauty of the place when I felt something against my back. I quickly turned and there, with a rifle pointing at my belly was a white man with a gray beard.

"Who are you and what are you doing here?" he asked.

He seemed taken aback a little when I answered in English.

"My name is Chingwe and I was born here. My mother planted this lily field and I have come to search for her and my father. They came here last year to gather bulbs and never returned."

"My name is Roush, Henry Roush. So it was your mother who planted these flowers here. I often wondered who did such a thing. She created a real beautiful place."

He lowered his rifle. "Come Chingwe, come on down to my cabin and let's talk a while."

At first I was apprehensive about this man, but by his friendly manner and the way he carried himself it soon became apparent that he had no intention of harming me in any way.

As we walked to his cabin he asked, "So you were born here?"

"Yes, in the little village below the falls. We called it Quenolapay Ohtenatit or Little Buck Town."

"My father Cahiktodo was once the village chief there. My mother was a Delaware named Chihopekelis or Bluebird. It was she who planted the lily field."

"My grandfather was a trader and Bluebird got the bulbs to plant here from a woman in Philadelphia years ago on a trip she made with my father to take furs and get supplies."

Henry said, "I was born over in Shenandoah County, Virginia. My brother Jacob was with Lewis's men at the Battle of Point Pleasant. He came home and all he could talk about was how beautiful it was here. After the Revolution me and my other brothers let him talk us into settling up here. It was a good move. This land is very fertile."

When they arrived at Henry's cabin Chingwe counted at least six children of various ages.

"You have many children Henry."

"This ain't all of 'em Chingwe. Me and Dorthea, my wife, have ten children living."

They were met by Henry's wife Dorthea at the door of the cabin.

"Dorthea, this here is Chingwe, he was born here. His mother is the one who planted the lily field."

Dorthea smiled at Chingwe and said. "Pleased to meet you Mr. Chingwe. You are welcome at our home. Can I fix you something to eat?"

Taken aback by the unexpected hospitality of this white family, Chingwe stuttered as he tried to reply.

"Dorthea," said Henry, "Just fetch us some of those biscuits we had for breakfast and some of that smoked ham."

"Come on Chingwe, let's go sit under the shade tree and talk a while."

Chingwe followed Henry to a shady spot beneath a large Maple tree. Henry leaned his rifle against the tree trunk and sat down motioning Chingwe to do the same.

"I'm afraid I have some bad news for you Chingwe. I believe I know where your mother is."

"A good while back I was working out in the fields when I heard a scream echoing through the hills. It was a sound that I had never heard the likes of before. It made the hair on the back of my neck stand up. I dropped my hoe, grabbed my rifle and ran back to the cabin as quick as I could fearing some wild creature was attacking my family. "

"As I got close to my cabin, I saw my wife and kids huddled together outside the cabin staring up into the woods. I sent them down to the falls where my oldest son and some others were building cabins. I told her to tell my son Michael to meet me at the lily field to find out what was happening."

"Dorthea, fearing an attack was about to happen, bid me not to go, but I figured if we was to come under attack it would have happened by now. I figured it was some kind of strange creature out there and I wanted to know what it was."

"I made my way towards the lily field and I heard that scream again. This time it was coming from down near the river. I started that way hoping I could see what made that terrible sound before it saw me."

"As I got close to the woods along the bank a strange looking man stepped out from the shadows and with his rifle cradled in his arms stood there, staring at me."

"I was no more that twenty feet from him. At first I was a little startled by his quick appearance from the brush. He was wearing buckskin that looked as dark as the night sky and he was covered with crimson blood. His hair was long, near to his waist. His face was covered red with blood too."

"I started walking towards him and asked, "Who are you? Are you all right? Did you see what was making that God awful sound?"

"He held up his hand and motioned for me to stop. Then he just stood there staring at me for what seemed like the longest minute. As I started towards him again he held up his hand and said, "Wetzel!"

"He turned and slipped back into the woods. By the time I made that twenty foot walk to where he was standing, there was no sign of him. It was like he melted into the woods and disappeared. I looked around for sign of which direction he went, but could find nothing."

"I decided to head back towards the lily field to meet up with my son Michael. He was standing on the edge of the field waiting for me."

"Pa, did you see what made that sound?"

"I told him of the strange apparition I had encountered down by the river and he wanted us to go look for this Wetzel feller."

"We decided to cut across the lily field and go into the woods and we started that way when we came upon a terrible sight."

"There, lying amidst the lilies, was the body of an Indian woman. Her throat had been slashed and her scalp was missing. It was then that I realized what had made that horrible sound, it had to have been that feller named Wetzel."

"The woman was wearing this around her neck Chingwe, do you recognize it?"

Henry held up a bobcat tooth that had been holed and strung on a beaded strip of rawhide.

Chingwe took the necklace and tears came to his eyes as he recognized the tooth that his father had given Bluebird years ago.

Dorthea approached with biscuits and ham and Henry motioned her away.

"Chingwe, I will let you be by yourself for a while. When you're ready, come on up to the cabin and then we'll eat and talk some more."

Chingwe drew his knees up to his chest and sat there with his head buried in hands as Henry took Dorthea by her arm and led her back towards the cabin.

"Let's just let him be for a while," he told her, "He just found out what happened to his mother."

Chapter Twenty One

The sun was beginning to set as Chingwe regained his composure and walked up to the cabin.

"Mr. Chingwe, I am so sorry for what happened to your mother." Dorthea said. "If there is anything we can do for you just say so and it will be done."

"Henry added, "Chingwe, you are more than welcome to stay here tonight. If you would like, I will take you to the lily field in the morning and show you where we buried your mother. We laid her beneath the ground where we found her."

"I thank you for your hospitality." Chingwe said. "I will stay."

After they ate a quiet supper Chingwe and Henry went outside to talk some more.

"My son Michael and some others from down in Virginia built a few cabins down where your village used to be Chingwe. Tomorrow I will take you down there if you'd like to go. There will be no trouble from my son and his family, but there are a few of those fellers down there that just don't take to Indians. Some of them lost loved ones back in 77. I'll make sure nothing happens to you."

"I would like to go Henry, just to see if anything of my village remains."

"What was the name of your village again?"

"We called it Quenolapay Ohtenatit, or Little Buck Town in English."

"They are calling it Letartsville now." Henry Said.

Chingwe looked at Henry with a surprised look on his face. "Letartsville? Letart was the name of my Grandfather."

"I didn't realize Letart was an Indian name." Henry said.

"It is not Indian. It is French. My grandfather was a Frenchman who had been adopted into the Shawnee tribe years ago. He once had a trading post across the river from the falls. My father's white name was also Letart, James Letart Jr. His Shawnee name was Cahiktodo."

"When my father was a small boy, my grandfather had his French name tattooed on his arm so he would never forget that he was half French and carried the name of his ancestors."

"Chingwe, then I'm afraid I have some more bad news for you. You see, they named the place Letartsville because about a week after we found your mother they found a man's body that had been washed over the falls and was caught in the brush along the shore. It was badly decomposed but on one of the arms you could see the word "Letart" tattooed there. The people decided to call the little town they were building Letartsville in honor of this unknown man. They even call the falls Letart's Falls. They made no connection with his body and your mother. They thought he was a white man."

"It is starting to make sense now. That wild man Wetzel must have killed them both that day and tossed your father's body into the river."

"Where is my father's body now?"

"They buried him down below the falls. We'll go down there in the morning. We'd best turn in now."

Chingwe slept outside. He refused to take shelter in the cabin saying it was too cramped up for him in there. He did take a blanket that was offered by Dorthea and slept beneath the maple tree.

Chingwe didn't get much sleep that night and when he did manage to doze off his dreams were filled with visions of his mother, his father and the little village that used to be.

He was already up when Henry emerged from the cabin and handed him several biscuits and a piece of smoked ham.

"Perhaps you should leave your rifle here Chingwe so's not to alarm some of the people down there. We'll go to Michael's cabin first. He and I will protect you."

Chingwe gobbled down his breakfast and they began their walk towards the cabins below the falls.

As the neared the cabin which Michael had built just below the falls, Michael was standing outside sharpening a scythe. He looked up and saw his father and Chingwe approaching.

The familiar sound of the water rushing over the falls came to Chingwe's ears and he fleetingly remembered his mother telling him that was the thing she missed most about their village.

A look of alarm and concern came to Michael's face as he noticed Chingwe's Indian garb. He laid down his scythe and walked forward to meet them.

"Good morning Michael. This is my new friend Chingwe, a Shawnee Indian. Chingwe was born here where we stand. He has come to search for his parents."

He went on to tell Michael about Bluebird and Cahiktodo. "Michael I want you to accompany us today as added protection for Chingwe."

"I will father, and Chingwe, I offer my condolences to you and your family."

Michael went into the cabin and came back out carrying his rifle and powder horn.

"Let's take a walk down the river bank and I will take you to where we buried your father."

"As they slowly walked, Chingwe would show them where a particular wigwam used to be and who lived there.

"This was where the longhouse once stood." He pointed out a spot and said, "And this was where my father's wigwam once was."

He told them of the life he had as a young boy in this place. He told them of his friends and the games they used to play. They all laughed when he told them of Toti's prank with the bearskin.

As they approached a cabin they were met by three men with rifles who demanded to know who this Indian was and why he was in their town.

"This is my friend Chingwe." Henry said, "He was born here and we are on the way to the grave of his father."

"Henry, do you expect us to believe that! Hell, he's probably just scoutin' the place out to set up an attack. There's probably more of 'em up there in the hills just waitin' for him to come back and tell 'em the layout of our town! I say we kill him now and dump him in the river then go up and find the rest of 'em."

"Calm down Jake, Chingwe's not here to scout for an attack. He came to find out what happened to his parents who came back here and never returned."

"So why does he need to come walking through Letartsville?"

"As I told you Jake, he was born here long before we came here. This used to be his village. His father was the village chief and you and I buried his father over there and named this town after him. Now show some respect for the son of the man whose name our town bears."

"That feller we buried was a white man named Letart. He weren't no injun! "

"My father was half French and half Shawnee", said Chingwe. Letart was his French name. His Shawnee name was Cahiktodo."

Jake was surprised that Chingwe spoke perfect English.

"If that's true, I want that half-breed dug up. That grave is next to my property and I don't want no stinkin' injun buried around me and my family. My brother, his wife and kids were murdered by you stinkin' savages up on the Greenbrier. Did you have anything to do with murderin' whites up the Kanawha? "

Chingwe answered with a question. "Did you have anything to do with murdering Indians on the Scioto?"

"Jake glared at Chingwe. "Don't let me catch you away from your friends there injun."

He turned and stalked away followed by the other two white men.

"Some people will never change," said Henry, "I feel sorry for Jake's loss but I know you and your people suffered losses too. It's a shame we can't all lay aside our differences and be at peace with one another."

Chingwe said, "My father told me that there would never be total peace between the white man and the Indians in my lifetime. I believe that to be true."

"Michael said, "I guess it is up to us to make a start at it so our children's children won't have to deal with such things."

They continued their walk to the grave of Cahiktodo. Someone had place a stone at the top of the grave and carved the name LETART on it.

"We'll leave you here alone for a moment Chingwe. We'll be just over there. When you're ready we'll go to the lily field to your mother's grave."

Chingwe soon rejoined them and they started for the lily field.

"I am worried," said Chingwe, "That white man Jake may try to dig up the grave of my father. I will remove him and place him next to my mother up in the lily field."

“Chingwe, you don’t have to do that.” Michael said, “Me and my sons will remove the body of your father and place him there.”

“Chingwe stopped and spoke. “What I say now comes straight from my heart. You, Michael and your father Henry are true friends. Your hearts are good. I have nothing but admiration for both of you. You have taken me in, me a Shawnee and once an enemy. You have shown mercy kindness and generosity. These are the traits that my father said is what makes a true man. I will always be indebted to you and you will always hold a special place in my heart.”

Henry replied, “My father, may he rest in peace, always held true to the principal that all men, regardless of their race are human beings. There are good and evil in all of them and we should never judge an individual because his race.”

“My father never held slaves and would often be found conversing with them whenever he visited someone who did. He enjoyed the stories they told. He believed that all human beings were basically the same and their actions with each other were determined by the way they were taught. His philosophy was to “Always strive to do good and never judge anyone else.” I have tried to instill these same principles in my children.”

They continued their walk

“My father, Cahiktodo, was a noted warrior and well respected by all the Shawnee and Delaware for his ferociousness in battle, but he often drew criticism for his merciful side. He especially hated the thought of killing women and children and he was very outspoken against the torture and murder of captives.”

“He was once accused of helping two female captives, who were to be burned at the stake, escape.

It was never proven, but knowing my father, I believe he did have something to do with it. He once told me that war makes men do things they would normally never even consider."

"Your father seems to have been a very intelligent man."

"Cahiktodo could speak and write fluently in French and English. He could speak the Algonquin language as well as the Iroquois tongue."

"So that is where you learned to speak the English language?" Michael asked.

"Yes, he taught my mother and me to converse in English and French as well as anyone else who wanted to learn."

Henry chuckled, "You know Chingwe, most of the white men I know can't even write their name yet they call all Indians "ignorant savages" when in fact they themselves are some of the most ignorant people in the world."

"You can never convince them otherwise and you can damn well argue from sunup to sundown on just about any subject and never be able to change their mind. My father always said "you cannot win an argument with ignorance."

They arrived at the edge of the lily field which was in full bloom. .

"Your mother is buried out there in the middle of the field Chingwe. Just walk that way and you will come upon her grave. We'll wait here for you."

Chingwe came upon his mother's grave and squatting down beside it he clutched the bobcat fang in his fist. He sang a song of remembrance as tears streamed down his face.

When he finished his song, his eye caught a flutter of blue. He quickly turned and saw a bluebird flying off just above the lily blooms.

Returning to Henry and his son he said, “I will be glad when my father’s remains are brought here to rest beside my mother. That white man said he didn’t want any Indians buried around him.”

“Little does he know that the spirits of my ancestors still inhabit these hills and valleys. We cannot see them nor can they see us, but they are here, enjoying a life of peace and tranquility beyond our understanding.”

“I will depart now”, said Chingwe, “But I would like to come back this fall and put lily bulbs on the graves of my parents. Would you mind?”

“Chingwe, you are always welcome here. Just be careful when you come. Come to my cabin or Michael’s first. We will get your father’s body up here and buried today.

“You be careful going to your home Chingwe.”

“I will my friends. Again I offer you my heartfelt thanks for all you have done for me. Peace be with you my friends.”

Chapter Twenty Two

"Did you return Grandfather?" Blue Feather asked.

"Yes, I did Blue Feather. And true to their word, my friends had moved the body of my father and laid it to rest beside my mother there in that field of lilies. They even carried the stone with the name Letart on it and placed it at the head of my father's grave. I dug up lily bulbs from around the edge of the field and planted them like my mother had taught me, all over my parent's graves."

"I have visited my friends several times since then. I brought my sons Ahanu and Pajackok to visit this place and see the lily field, just as I have brought you now. I was going to bring my little Nuttah but she caught the white man's fever and died the winter before."

"Early tomorrow morning I will go to my friend Henry's cabin and ask his permission to take you children to visit the graves of your great grandparents and see the lily field that Bluebird created."

"Is that mean white man Jake still there" Gray Squirrel asked.

"I do not know if he is still living. I am not even sure if my friend Henry is still living. They would be quite old by now."

"If Henry is not there I will go to the cabin of his son Michael. We must be cautious for there are undoubtedly still some whites there who carry hatred for Indians in their hearts and who might try to do us harm."

Before the sun came up the next morning, the children helped Chingwe carry the canoe from its hiding place down to the river's edge.

Chingwe climbed aboard and the children pushed him off into the current. He waved at them and said, "I will return this evening before dark."

Chingwe paddled the canoe out into the current and at an angle made his way across the river to the Ohio side. Beaching his canoe near the big rock he called Sikona Yapewi. He struggled to get his canoe out of the water and up into the brush.

Working his way up the bank he stumbled on a rock and fell, tearing a hole in his leggings. He sat there for a moment and reflected on his past.

"When I was young, I could run up and down these hills like they were nothing. Now I am old and even trying to walk up this bank is difficult. Oh! To have my youth back one more time!"

He remembered his friends Toti and White Hawk. Toti was killed on a raid up the Kanawha and his friend White Hawk was killed at the Battle of the Thames.

"Are their spirits here now?" he thought. He closed his eyes and could hear their laughter as they dove off the big rock into the swirling waters of the Spaylawetheepi.

"I am glad they can't see me struggling to get up this bank."

Chingwe finally made it to the top of the bank and the walking was easier as he headed for Henry's cabin. The sun came up and the air was filled with the chirping of many birds. To Chingwe it was if they were welcoming him home.

As he approached Henry's cabin he was greeted by two big redbone coon hounds. With their tails wagging and baying loudly they rushed towards Chingwe.

A boy, who Chingwe recognized as Daniel, rushed out of the cabin and called the dogs. He came up to Chingwe and said, "Chingwe, it's good to see you, why Grandfather was just talking about you last night. He was wondering if you would ever come pay us a visit again. Come on in, he will be so glad to see you."

Chingwe followed Daniel into the cabin and there was Henry sitting at the kitchen table eating some fried eggs and biscuits. Henry stood up, almost knocking the chair over and hugged his old friend.

"Where have you been Chingwe? Haven't seen you for a coon's age. Thought maybe you might have died or something! Here, sit down and have some breakfast with us."

"Dorthea, look who's here!'

Dorthea came out of the kitchen area wiping her hands on her apron. "Why Chingwe, it's good to see you."

"Fry him up some eggs Dorthea and some of that ham."

"It is good to see you Henry, Dorthea. It has been quite some time. How are things with you and your family? How is Michael? "

"All are doing well Chingwe. By the way, the name of the town has changed. People stopped calling it Letartsville and now it is just known as Letart Falls."

"The area where Michael's cabin is and down below the falls is called Buck Town. Michael started calling it that after you told him of thc village there and the name sort of stuck. Now everybody's calling that area Buck Town. How's things with your family?"

"My wife passed away two years ago Henry. Life for my people has not been good. We have had to move several times. From our village on the Scioto, to the Mad River and then up on the Miami."

"I made friends with a white man who allowed me and my family to live back down on the Scioto but now he wants us to move so he can sell the land. It is not good to be an Indian in the Ohio Country."

"I have brought my grandchildren Henry, to see the place where their ancestors once lived and are buried. I want them to see the lily field that my mother created. I ask your permission to do this."

"Chingwe you don't have to ask my permission for anything. Of course you can bring your grandchildren here. You can bring them anytime you want. Why, if you and your family want to move back here I will give you some land up near the lily field."

"Henry, I am honored by your offer, but I don't feel we would be welcomed here by most people. Me, my sons and their families have decided to move west to Missouri to join those of us who have already moved there. We will try to make a life for our children there. This will be my last visit to this place."

"Chingwe, I am sorry to hear that, but I wish you and your family well. Maybe it will be a good thing. Your sons will have a chance of raising their children away from the bigotry that seems to dwell in these lands now. I just hope you have made the right choice."

"I want you to remember Chingwe, you and your family are always welcome here. If you ever want to come back my offer will still be good. I will make sure my sons honor it also."

Chingwe spent the rest of the day with the Roush family and as the evening sun touched the top of the hills, he bade everyone goodbye.

"I will take my grandchildren to visit the lily field at sunrise in the morning and we will leave from there before the sun reaches midway to the top of the sky. Farewell my friends."

"Farewell to you Chingwe may you and your family find the peace and happiness you deserve."

Chapter Twenty Three

It was almost dark when Chingwe beached the canoe on the Virginia side. He was greeted by his grandchildren who helped him pull the canoe out of the water and return it to its hiding place.

"Children, have you eaten yet?"

"Yes grandfather. We saved some turkey for you."

"I will eat and then we must retire for the evening. We will be up before sunrise tomorrow. My friend has given me permission to take you children to see the lily field and visit the graves of your ancestors. When we leave there tomorrow, we will return to our home on the Scioto."

Chingwe looked out across the Ohio and noticed fog starting to form above the water. A cool, gentle wind caused it to swirl just above the surface.

About an hour before dawn, Chingwe woke the children. The air was filled with a thick fog making it hard to see more than a few feet. A cool front had moved into the area causing the fog to rise from the river and fill the valley.

"Shouldn't we wait until the fog clears?" Dark Sky asked.

"I know the way." Chingwe answered. "I have traveled in this type of fog many times before."

After a quick breakfast he had the boys take down the shelter. The hides were dripping wet from the fog in the air. They carried all their supplies down to where the canoe was hidden in the brush. Slipping and sliding in the wet grass, Chingwe had them hide their supplies in the brush.

"We will come back for this before we head home."

They moved the canoe down to the water's edge and the Blue Feather climbed in first.

"Why are you taking that basket?" asked Chingwe.

“Because, Grandfather, I want to dig up some of the lily bulbs and take them with us.”

“Now is not the time to do that. That should be done in the fall.”

“I know Grandfather, but you said this is the only time we will be here and I won’t have another chance to get them. I will take care of them just like Bluebird. I will keep them moist, not wet. I will care for them just like Bluebird.”

Chingwe climbed in next followed by the two boys. As they paddled out into the swirling mist Blue Feather said. “I wish I could have known Bluebird.”

“She would have loved you Blue Feather. Sometimes when I look at you I can see her in your features, hear her in your voice. The way you carry yourself reminds me of my mother.”

Gray Squirrel called out, “Grandfather, I cannot see the big rock! I cannot see anything!”

“It’s right there in front of you. You will see it soon.”

“I haven’t lost my touch.” Chingwe thought to himself as the rock emerged from the swirling fog.

“There it is Gray Squirrel, just as I said. There is Sikona Yapewi right in front of you.”

Chingwe guided the canoe upon the shore near the rock and they climbed out. They pulled the canoe up and hid it in the brush. The children helped their Grandfather up the bank this time and he was grateful for it.

The fog seemed thicker at the top of the bank and Chingwe had to stop for a moment to get his bearings.

“We go this way” he said, “Follow me.”

They made their way through the brush and grasses which were covered with moisture. They had not gone very far before their clothing was soaked.

The sun was starting to come up over the hills and the light filtering down through the fog seemed to make it harder to see. Chingwe knew where he was though and kept the children behind him as they made their way.

After a while, Chingwe motioned for his grandchildren to stop. He told them to sit down beside him.

He raised his arm and pointed.

"There just in front of you is the lily field. When the sun comes up and burns away the fog you will see a sight like you have never seen before."

A cool breeze brushed their faces as they sat staring into the fog in anticipation. The breeze picked up causing the fog to swirl in front of them. The sunlight began filtering through the fog and soon the edge of the field became visible.

Blue Feather could contain herself no longer. She jumped up and ran over to a patch of purple lilies that appeared out of the rising mist.

"Grandfather, Oh Grandfather!" She called out excitedly, "Look! These flowers are so beautiful!"

She fell down on her knees and tried to smell the flowers.

The lily's petals were dripping water from the heavy fog and made her nose wet.

"Oh look Grandfather", she said sadly, "Look! They are crying...crying for Bluebird."

The fog quickly lifted exposing the entire field which was aflame with colors. Reds, Yellows, Blues, Whites, Pinks, Purples and multi-colored lilies of all kinds and shapes. The fog in the air was replaced by their sweet perfume.

Chingwe and the boys joined Blue Feather and he led them through the lilies to the middle of the field.

"Here beneath our feet, lay the remains of Bluebird and Cahiktodo, my father and mother."

He stood before the rock that had the name Letart carved on it. There were no discernible signs of any type of grave, just the stone. Long ago, Chingwe had planted bulbs over the graves of his parents and the lilies had taken over.

Chingwe and the children sang the song of remembrance and then they walked through the field looking at all the different kinds of lilies.

They were surprised when a fine buck deer with three does and a fawn emerged from the woods near them and began feeding on the grasses near the edge of the lily field. The deer paid no attention to them. The buck looked up a few times and stared at them, but made no effort to run away.

The boys soon tired of looking at flowers and asked Chingwe if they could go down to the river to explore. He reluctantly agreed but warned them to be alert for sign of someone approaching.

Chingwe sat down beneath a tree that was growing near the middle of the field and leaning back against its trunk he watched his young granddaughter scurrying around amid the flowers.

"Look at this one Grandfather! She exclaimed. "It's so beautiful. Oh and look here at this red one and this blue one! Which one is your favorite Grandfather? I love them all! I love this place Grandfather! I want to plant a lily field just like this, just like Bluebird did."

As he sat there smiling at his granddaughter and her enthusiasm, he was startled by a whir of blue. He was amazed when a bluebird landed on his leg and sat there with its head cocked sideways, looking him right in the eye. The bluebird chirped and took off flying towards Blue Feather.

The bluebird flew around Blue Feather's head a few times then landed near her feet and began chirping.

Blue Feather, startled at first, knelt and held out her hand. The bluebird hopped upon her wrist and as Blue Feather rose and turned to show her Grandfather, it jumped upon her shoulder.

"Look Grandfather, Look, it's the spirit of Bluebird! She's trying to talk to me but I don't understand her!"

Chingwe was up on his feet by this time, staring in wonder at the sight before him.

"I have heard of these things!" He thought to himself.

"Child! Don't listen with your ears! Listen with your heart and your mind. Don't talk, just close your eyes and listen, then you will understand her words."

He sat back down and watched as a smile came across Blue Feather's face. She opened her eyes and turned back to the lilies.

With the Bluebird balanced on her shoulder she walked through the lilies, stopping now and then to stoop and dig up a bulb. She soon had her basket full.

The bluebird flew off her shoulder and back towards Chingwe. It landed beside him, looked at him again and flew away into the woods.

Blue Feather came up to her grandfather lugging her basket now heavy with bulbs.

"Grandfather, she told me which bulbs to dig up and where I could find moss to wrap them in. I will set the basket here and go get the moss. She told me how to keep them moist and said that they will flower for me. I will be right back."

Blue Feather went scurrying towards the river where her brothers were.

Chingwe grinned as he wiped a tear from his cheek.

"It is true." he thought to himself, *"The spirits of my ancestors still inhabit this place and I will*

someday come back myself to join them. We will all, once again live in peace below the falls in the little village of Quenolapay Ohtenatit."

Separating Fact from Fiction

Chapter One

James and Ann Letort were real people who actually lived. James Letort was the son of a French Huguenot who came to British America to escape Catholic persecution in his native country. He, his wife and brothers were some of the first Indian traders to set up business in Pennsylvania. He was once under suspicion of dealing with the French and brought before the Council at Philadelphia. He was jailed and was later released after paying security of 1000 pounds.

From Colonial Records of Philadelphia:

1703 – James Letort left Lancaster County Pa for Canada in 1701. In 1703 he was brought before Council and Magistrates to be examined and no great occasion was found to expect him of evil designs against the government, him having been bred into it from his infancy and behaved himself hitherto well. He was seduced to depart in 1701 in time of peace by the instigation of some others, nevertheless as he is now come back it was thought wise to bring him before council to explain his action.

1704 – James Letort in jail at Philadelphia. He wrote council that he had "always been faithful and bore true allegiance to the Crown of England, and was ready to give such further security as should be thought reasonable." On October 31st., he was brought before the council and his petition was considered. The council ordered that "unless James Letort can give sufficient security for his good behavior in the sum of 1000 pounds, to be produced at the next setting of the council, he shall still be detained as a prisoner."

The West Jersey Trading Company did exist however it is fiction that it had any of the Letort family in its employ.

Adam Miller is fictional.

The rest of the chapter is fiction.

Chapter Two

Chingwe and his grandchildren are fictional.

Sikona Yapewi, the big rock does exist. The name is fictional. The rock is along the river just above the present village of Antiquity in Meigs County, Ohio. I have heard old timers talk of the Indian carvings that used to be on that rock. Time and the river itself have eroded these drawings.

Toti and White Hawk are fictional.

The falls actually existed as well as rapids above and below them.

The falls were located on the Ohio side of the river just below where Letart Island is located today. In 1796 George Collot made a map of the Ohio River and he shows two Islands near present day Letart Falls. In the area just below the falls (He wrote Tart Falls) he made a sounding and the water level went from 20 feet to 8 feet in a very short distance. He noted: "Dangerous place when the water is low."

In 1770 George Washington traveled the Ohio River and made notes in a journal. He referred the entire area of the "Boot of Ohio" as the "Great Bent" area. He noted in his Journal about Old Town Creek:

Six miles below this comes in a small creek on the west side at the end of a small naked island and just above another pavement of rocks. This creek comes thro a bottom of fine land, & opposite to it (On the East side of the River) appears to be large bottom of very fine land also. At this place begins what they call the Great Bent 5 miles below this again, on the east side comes in (about 200 yds. above a little stream or gut) another creek which is just below an island, on the upper point of which there are some dead standing trees, and a parcel of white bodied Sycamores. In the mouth of this creek lyes a Sycamore blown down by the wind. From hence an East line may be run 3 or 4 miles; Thence a north line till it strikes the river, which I apprehend would include 3 or 4000 of exceedingly valuable land. At the mouth of this creek which is 3 or 4 miles above two islands (at the lower end of the last is a rapid & the point of the bend) is the Warrior's Trail to the Cherokee country. For two miles and half below this the river runs a No. Et. Course & finished what they call the Great Bent. Two mile an a half below this again we encamped.

The trading post of James Letart (son of James and Ann Letort) was real and located somewhere across the river from the falls in what is now present Mason County, West Virginia. The village of Letart, West Virginia bears his name. James had a brother named Jacques Letort who had a trading post near what is now Ravenswood in Jackson County, West Virginia.

Pahcotai Koona, Autumn Snow, wife of the trader James Letart, did exist but in this novel her name is fictional. Her real name has been lost to history. According to Don Greene, Shawnee history researcher, James was adopted into the Shawnee nation. His wife is recorded only as "a Shawnee woman."

The village of Quenolapay Ohtenatit or Little Buck Town did exist just below the falls. The name is fictional. Quenolapay Ohtenatit can be translated from the Algonquin language as Little Buck Town. As long as I can remember the area along the river and just below Letart Island in present day Letart Falls, Ohio, has always been referred to as Buck Town. The village was shared by people from both the Lenape (Delaware) and Shawnee nations. Both tribes were of the Algonquin linguistic group and the Shawnee considered the Delaware as their Grandfathers.

James Letart Jr. or Cahiktodo did exist. He was the son of James Letart and the Shawnee woman. The name Cahiktodo is real. I have been unsuccessful in obtaining the English translation of this name from the many Shawnee sources I have contacted. According to Shawnee history, Cahiktodo was a "Métis" (may-tee) or half French and half Shawnee. He married a Delaware woman and was a village chief. He is recorded as taking part in the Battle of Point Pleasant and raids on settlements up the Kanawha River.

Chihopekelis or Bluebird, wife of Cahiktodo did exist, but her name in this novel is fictional. Again it has been lost to history. She is recorded in Shawnee history as being slain by Lewis Wetzel.

Raids into the country of their old enemies the Cherokee did take place and the Warrior's Trail to the Cherokee Country began very close to the falls as stated in George Washington's journal.

The rest of the chapter is fiction.

Chapter Three

The **French and Indian War** did happen. Most of the nations in the Ohio Country and Pennsylvania including the Shawnee and Delaware took sides with the French at first. After the fall of Fort Duquesne, the British were successful in convincing them to withdrawal their allegiance to France and most of the tribes declared neutrality. The British made promises to the tribes that they had no intention of keeping, such as the abandonment of Fort Duquesne, which they renamed Fort Pitt, and withdrawal of the military from western Pennsylvania. They also promised to stop the encroachment of settlers onto land claimed by the nations. They said they would only allow traders to go into Indian lands.

The French and Indian victory over General Braddock actually happened and is known in history as "Braddock's Defeat."

The attack on Fort Duquesne by General Forbes actually happened as well as the foolish advance of his officer, Major Grant.

The rest of the chapter is fiction.

Chapter Four

The Delaware and Shawnee had houses called wigwams. They were not like the wigwams and tepees of the plains Indians. The houses were usually made of cut young trees with their bases buried in the ground. The tops were bent over and tied together making a frame. The frame was covered with sheets of bark usually from Elm or Chestnut trees.

The Couriers for James Letort the trader, Jean Lebeau and Christopher Burkey are fictional.

The **Palisades** section of the river did exist. The area referred to is located between the present day village of Reedsville and Hockingport, Ohio and can be seen while traveling on Ohio State Route 124 between the villages. Of course it looks much different today than it did back in the frontier days. The dams that have affected the water levels, the roads and natural erosion of the river have changed it.

Flocks of Passenger Pigeons as described did exist and according to the Smithsonian Encyclopedia they were recorded by many early explorers:

Early explorers and settlers frequently mentioned passenger pigeons in their writings. Samuel de Champlain in 1605 reported "countless numbers," Gabriel Sagard-Theodat wrote of "infinite multitudes," and Cotton Mather described a flight as being about a mile in width and taking several hours to pass overhead.

Daniel Greathouse and Bill Grills did exist. Greathouse was a villainous and notorious character of the frontier. It was Greathouse who was responsible for the murder of Mingo Chief Logan's family and his actions directly caused Lord Dunmore's War and the deaths of many settlers in Virginia and Western Pennsylvania.

The rest of the chapter is fiction.

Chapter Five

Simon Girty did exist. His interaction with Cahiktodo is fictional. Simon Girty was hated by the white settlers as much as he was revered by the Indian nations. As a young teenager he and his brothers were captured by Delaware Indians. He was given to the Seneca nation which adopted him. His brothers were adopted into the Delaware and Shawnee nations.

Simon Girty attempted to rejoin the whites but was treated badly by the British and the white population in general. He saw through the British façade and realized they wanted total control of the Indians and were intent in obtaining their lands by deceit or whatever means necessary to open it for settlement. He gave up his employment as an interpreter for the British and went back to the Seneca nation.

At the beginning of the American Revolution, Simon first joined the American Colonists in their fight for freedom from the British, but soon realized their intentions as far as expanding settlement. It was worse for the Indians than the British. He figured the Indian nations would have a better chance of negotiating with the British so he flipped back to their side.

The Seneca, including the Ohio Seneca were members of the Six Nation Iroquois Confederation and known as the "Guardians of the Western Door." Girty was an adopted Seneca but led war parties made up mostly of Algonquin speaking warriors from the Ohio Country and western Pennsylvania. The Americans considered him a renegade but the Indians highly respected him and listened to his counsel.

Lewis Wetzel did exist. If Lewis Wetzel were alive today he would be classified as an insane, psychopathic, murdering serial killer. In his day he was often held as a hero by some. His soul reason for living was to kill Indians. It mattered not to him whether they were peaceful Indians, men, women or children. He was responsible for the deaths of over a hundred Indians. He was able to do this because he was considered the best woodsman that ever lived. According to James Pierce, author of "Lewis Wetzel, Dark Hero of the Ohio," "*He was probably the best single combat fighter European-America ever produced.*" His habit of letting out a blood curdling, hair raising scream each time he killed an Indian earned him the title of "The Death Wind". This was what the Indians of the Ohio Country and western Pennsylvania called him.

Henry Weber and the rest of the chapter are fiction.

Chapter Six

This method of fishing is still used to this day.

Spaylawetheepi is the Shawnee name for the Ohio River.

The Shawnee and Delaware didn't eat much fried food. Usually they baked, boiled or broiled their meat. However, with the introduction of iron skillets from traders, I'm sure they enjoyed a few fried delicacies also.

The rest of the chapter is fiction.

Chapter Seven

Oxen were the preferred animals to pull heavy wagons.

Furs and pelts were like money in the early frontier. As a matter of fact, the American dollar is sometimes called a Buck because after the American Revolution, when America started creating its own money; one dollar was the usual payment for the hide of a deer or buckskin.

The places mentioned in the journey to Philadelphia really existed. The journey itself is fictional.

Chapter Eight

Wharton Street in **Philadelphia** existed.

Joseph and Anne Miller, their children and servants are fictional.

The rest of the chapter is fiction.

Chapter Nine

The list of supplies is made up of actual items on a supply list from an early trader.

The **Eastern Cougar** was often called a Panther, Panter or Painter by frontiersmen.

The rest of the chapter is fiction.

Chapter Ten

Ottawa Chief **Pontiac** and Seneca Chief Kiashuta joined forces to gather tribes to force the British into living up to their promises they failed to keep after the French and Indian War. The ensuing conflict became known as Pontiac's Rebellion.

The rest of this chapter is fiction.

Chapter Eleven

Logan and his village existed. His relationship with Christopher Burkey and the Letart family is fictional.

The Mingo warriors Genesee and Kaske are fictional.

The three islands mentioned existed. They were sometimes called the Brother Islands.

Greathouse's ambush of the flotilla is fictional, but if anyone would have done such a thing, he would have been the one to do it.

Grills existed and was a constant companion of Greathouse until the massacre of Logan's family.

Baker is a fictional character.

The war that broke out between the nations and the British that Chingwe mentions is Pontiac's Rebellion.

The massacre of Logan's family by Daniel Greathouse did occur. Logan always blamed Michael Cresap for the slaughter of his family. Cresap had led several raids against Indian villages he thought were hostile to the settlers but it was Daniel Greathouse that perpetrated the massacre at Yellow Creek. Logan gathered warriors from the Mingo, Shawnee and Delaware. He began a series of revenge seeking attacks on settlers in both western Pennsylvania and Virginia. This prompted Lord Dunmore, Governor of Virginia to declare war on the Shawnee and Mingo nations.

The rest of the chapter is fiction.

Chapter Twelve

The **lily field** created by Bluebird is fictional.

Snowsnake was a game played by children of both Algonquin and Iroquoian nations.

Pahsaheman is a Delaware game and was played as explained in the novel. The size of the ball ranged anywhere from the size of a modern softball to a volley ball.

The rest of this chapter is fiction.

Chapter Thirteen

Pontiac's Rebellion ended in failure but they did get the British promise that no white settlers would be permitted to occupy land in the Ohio Country. Of course the British had no intention of keeping their word. Cantukee or present day Kentucky was held sacred by the Indian nations in the Ohio Country and the Cherokees to the south. No tribe was permitted to take up residence there, but all were free to use the area as a hunting ground and for salt gathering. The tribes, especially Shawnee took great offense when white settlers, some led by Daniel Boone through the Cumberland Gap, began to settle there.

Settlers from the north and east who were headed for Kentucky generally traveled there by flatboat. **Flatboats** were being built to specifications at Fort Pitt. They ranged in size from 8 feet wide and 20 feet long to 20 feet wide and 100 feet long. Flatboats were rectangular in shape and generally had boarded up sides of 2 to 3 feet high. There was usually a shed on the back side for the livestock and a small cabin near the middle or in the front for sleeping. They were sometimes called Kentucky Boats or Broadhorns. To move these boats through the water, the settlers relied on the current of the river and long oar shaped poles on both sides called "sweeps." There was a rudder in the rear and in the front was a short oar known as a "Gouger". In the front of the boat was a large reel loaded with strong rope called a "hawser" When needed, the rope could be tied to a tree on shore and the boat "reeled" in.

Flatboats were built to travel only with the current. Upon reaching their destination, the settlers would disassemble the boat and use the wood in building their cabins. It was very difficult to maneuver these boats especially through the rapids near Letart Falls. At times, especially when the river was running low, it was treacherous for even a canoe to pass through those rapids. Allen Eckert, author of "The Frontiersman", mentions in his book that the famed frontiersman Simon Kenton almost met his end there on those waters.

Chapter Fourteen

Dunmore's force moved to **Fort Pitt** then down river to the mouth of the Hocking River where he built a small fortification and named it Fort Gower. The original plan of attack was for Col. Andrew Lewis's forces to remain at Point Pleasant. Dunmore's forces would travel down river attacking and burning villages along the river to meet up with Lewis at the point. From there the two forces would travel on down river and up the Scioto to attack the villages there.

While at Fort Gower, Dunmore decided to alter the battle plans. He sent a message to Lewis that he would not be joining him at Point Pleasant but would instead move overland to attack the villages on the Scioto. He ordered Lewis to cross the Ohio River and join him there. The Indians attacked Lewis and his men before this order could be carried out.

The Indian forces, having failed in their effort to destroy Lewis's force at **Point Pleasant**, retreated back to their villages on the Scioto. Cornstalk, at the

Shawnee town of Chalawgatha, sent a message to the approaching Dunmore asking for peace negotiations. Dunmore agreed to meet with the Indians beneath a very large Elm tree near the village which was about 7 miles from present day Circleville, Ohio. It was here that Logan gave his famous speech. Dunmore dispatched messages to Lewis ordering him to refrain from attacking while he made peace with the Indians. This infuriated Lewis who was intent on raining destruction upon the enemy. At the meeting a treaty was drawn up and the Indians gave up their rights to all of Kentucky and Virginia. They agreed that the Ohio River would be the boundary between the Indian lands and white settlement. Not all of the Indians of the Ohio Country were happy with this agreement, especially Logan who refused to sign the treaty.

The destruction of the villages at Old Town and Letart Falls has never been recorded but it is a distinct possibility that their destruction came at the hands of Dunmore's forces. Although the villages were not major towns, Dunmore had to know of their existence as he had messengers and scouts traveling up and down the river between Fort Gower and Lewis's forces at Point Pleasant. The sole purpose of the expedition in the first place was to wage war and destroy all the Indian's villages and crops in the Ohio Country.

Pekuwe was a major Shawnee Indian town and named after the Pekuwe Sept of the Shawnee Tribe.

Pucksinwah was a Chief and the father of the great Shawnee warrior Tecumseh. He was killed at the Battle of Point Pleasant.

The relationship between Pucksinwah and Cahiktodo is fiction.

The rest of the chapter is fiction.

Chapter Fifteen

Chiksika was the oldest son of Pucksinwah and a great influence on the early life of Tecumseh, his younger brother. Chiksika was killed in an attack on Buchanan's Station near present day Nashville, Tennessee during the American Revolution.

The rest of this chapter is fiction.

Chapter Sixteen

At the peace council, held under a huge **Elm** tree, Logan gave his famous speech sometimes called "Logan's Lament" This is the actual English translation of his speech.

The great fight Chingwe is talking about is the American Revolution.

The murder of Cornstalk at Point Pleasant actually happened.

The rest of this chapter is fiction.

Chapter Seventeen

After the murder of Cornstalk at Fort Randolph, The Shawnee, Delaware and other Ohio Country tribes united with the British and stepped up their **attacks on settlers** in Virginia and Kentucky.

Palawi and Okowellos are fictional.

The attack on the settlers on the Kanawha by Cahiktodo is fictional but based on actual events.

It is a misconception that all Indians of the early American frontier were brutal, savages that tortured raped and murdered innocent whites. There were many American Indians who were against such things. Tecumseh, for one, as a young boy witnessed the burning of a prisoner and it disgusted him. He told his friends that if any of them ever partook in such a thing he would disown them. The American Indians were fully capable of extending kindness and mercy to their enemies as evidenced by the adoption of many white prisoners into their tribes and their refusal to be repatriated back into white society. Even the great American frontiersmen Daniel Boone and Simon Kenton were once adopted into the Shawnee nation.

There were white men who were just as savage and brutal as any Indian ever portrayed as being such. To name a few, Daniel Greathouse, perpetrator of the Yellow Creek Massacre, David Williamson, perpetrator of the Gnadenhutten Massacre and Lewis Wetzel, murder of over a hundred men, women and children.

There were good and bad in both races. Simon Girty stood up for Simon Kenton when he was made to run the Gauntlet several times and was sentenced to die by burning at the stake. Simon Kenton and

Chief Logan of the Mingo were instrumental in saving him from the stake and his ultimate adoption into the Shawnee nation. Simon Girty also protested to the Delaware concerning their revenge burning of Colonel Crawford for the atrocities at Gnadenhutten. He had to stop his efforts to save Crawford when he himself was threatened with loss of status with the Delaware and possible death.

The rest of the chapter is fiction.

Chapter Eighteen

In 1777 the Indian attacks on the settlements up the Kanawha and New River in Virginia and on the settlements in Kentucky were at its height. This year became known as the **"Year of the Bloody Sevens."**

The three hundred horsemen were Kentucky militiamen who attacked and partially burned the old town of Chawlagotha (Chillicothe) near present day Circleville, Ohio.

Fort Laurens was located in present day Tuscarawas County, Ohio and was the only American fortification in the Ohio country during the American Revolution.

Kanti, Ahanu, Pajackok, Nuttah and Oota Dabun are fictional characters

The narrative on the efforts of Tecumseh and his brother Tenskatawa are factual.

Chapter Nineteen

The **split** of the Shawnee nation did occur with many people from all the Septs moving west to escape the encroaching white settlers.

It is recorded in Shawnee history that the wife of Cahiktodo was murdered by Lewis Wetzel. The murder of Cahiktodo by Wetzel is not proven but is possible and the explanation for the legend of the body of a Frenchman with the word Letart tattooed on his arm found below the falls seems plausible. However the actual murders depicted in this novel are fictional.

The rest of the chapter is fiction.

Chapter Twenty

Henry, Dorthea and Michael Roush did exist. However the relationship between Chingwe and the Roush family is fictional.
The rest of the chapter is fiction.

Chapter Twenty One

This chapter is all fiction.

Chapter Twenty Two

This chapter is all fiction.

Chapter Twenty Three

This chapter is all fiction.

Quotations

Tecumseh 1790

"No people are all bad, just as none are all good."

Tecumseh 1791

"We have good reason not to trust the Americans, but I am by no means convinced we do not have a sufficiency of cause to mistrust the British as well. Their past actions have shown us that they do only that which most supports their own aims and desires. They say they are our friends, but sometimes we must watch friends even more closely than enemies."

Tecumseh 1795

"Sell a country! Why not sell the air, the great sea, as well as the earth? Did not the Great Spirit make them all for the use of his children?"

Tecumseh 1808

“If the Indian loves, he speaks the truth; but if he does not, he is silent."

Tecumseh

"A single twig breaks, but the bundle is strong. Someday I will embrace our brother tribes and draw them into a bundle and together we will win our country back."

Tecumseh to William Henry Harrison 1810

"The President may sit still in his town and drink his wine, while you and I have to fight it out."

Tecumseh

"Where today are the Pequot? Where are the Narragansett, the Mohican, the Pokanoket, and many other once powerful tribes of our people? They have vanished before the avarice and the oppression of the White Man, as snow before a summer sun.

"Will we let ourselves be destroyed in our turn without a struggle, give up our homes, our country bequeathed to us by the Great Spirit, the graves of our dead and everything that is dear and sacred to us? I know you will cry with me, 'Never! Never!"

Chiksika, Brother of Tecumseh

"The whole white race is a monster who is always hungry, and what he eats is land."

Blue Jacket 1791

"Your words circle like soaring birds which never land. I will try to catch them and take them back for my people to hear."

Moses Shongo, Seneca Medicine Man

"Free yourself from negative influence. Negative thoughts are the old habits that gnaw at the roots of the soul."

Shawnee Chief Yellow Hawk 1775

"They insult us and our wives and our children and our way of life. We are losing our dignity, our self-respect. Why must it be we who turn our backs and walk away when it is we who are injured? Why may we not, as we always have, repay in kind what we receive at the hands of our enemies?"

Seneca Chief Red Jacket

"Brother, you say there is but one way to worship and serve the Great Spirit. If there is but one religion, why do you white people differ so much about it? Why not all agreed, as you can all read the Book?"

Col. Henry Bouquet to General Amherst 1763

"I will try to inoculate (with Smallpox) the Indians by means of blankets that may fall in their hands, taking care however not to get the disease myself. As it is pity to oppose good men against them, I wish we could make use of the Spaniard's Method, and hunt them with English Dogs. Supported by Rangers, and some Light Horse, who would I think, effectively extirpate or remove that vermin.

General Jeffrey Amherst to Col. Henry Bouquet 1763

"You will do well to try to inoculate the Indians by means of blankets, as well as to try every other method that can serve to extirpate this execrable race. I should be very glad your scheme for hunting

them down by dogs could take effect, but England is at too great a distance to think of that at present."

General Phil Sheridan 1869

"The only good Indians I ever saw were dead."

Theodore Roosevelt 1886

"I suppose I should be ashamed to say that I take the Western view of the Indian. I don't go so far as to think that the only good Indians are dead Indians, but I believe nine out of every ten are, and I shouldn't like to inquire too closely into the case of the tenth."

Grand Council Of American Indians 1927

"The white people, who are trying to make us over into their image, they want us to be what they call "assimilated," bringing the Indians into the mainstream and destroying our own way of life and our own cultural patterns. They believe we should be contented like those whose concept of happiness is materialistic and greedy, which is very different from our way.

We want freedom from the white man rather than to be integrated. We don't want any part of the establishment, we want to be free to raise our children in our religion, in our ways, to be able to hunt and fish and live in peace. We don't want power, we don't want to be congressmen, or bankers....we want to be ourselves. We want to have our heritage, because we are the owners of this land and because we belong here.

The white man says there is freedom and justice for all. We have had "freedom and justice," and that is why we have been almost exterminated. We shall not forget this."

About the Author

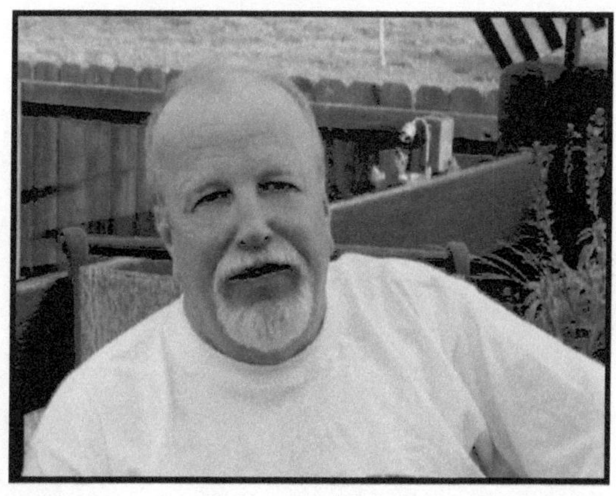

C. Stephen Badgley or Steve, as he is prefers to be called, is a lover of history, especially early American History. He has held this love ever since he was first introduced to Ohio History by his Fifth Grade teacher, Mrs. Augusta Barnhart in the town of Tuppers Plains, Ohio and that was fifty years ago.

He has a "special" fascination for the French and Indian War era and has read many books and manuscripts on the subject.

Steve is a combat veteran of the Viet Nam War, serving as a Corpsman with the 26th Marines.

He was born near the village of Letart Falls in Meigs County, Ohio and is the author of another historical / fiction novel titled "*Arcadia.*" He is now working a third novel entitled "*Opequon*" and hopes to have it finished soon.

The Cover Artist

Mary Louise Holt

The work of this Cincinnati native and wonderful artist spans various genres including Historical, Wildlife, portraits and landscape. Her works are primarily created in oils on canvas following in the footsteps of master artists who have gone before.

"I love nature in all its varied forms. Because of this, I enjoy painting creatures large and small as well as landscapes, florals and even the human form...past and present. My goal as an artist is to create beautiful images filled with natural light and lush color that give the collector a sense of the beauty I see as an artist. I also hope my artwork will give the collector pleasure for many years to come."

Mary Lou Holt

To view Mary Lou's works, please visit her website at:

www.marylouiseholt.com

For more great stories visit our web site at:

WWW.BadgleyPublishingCompany.com

Badgley Publishing Company

Thank You

www.ingramcontent.com/pod-product-compliance
Lightning Source LLC
Chambersburg PA
CBHW020443270626
47155CB00022B/1369

* 9 7 8 0 9 8 5 4 4 0 3 6 7 *